# Destiny of Ukrainian Girl

*by*

Kishan Lal Sharma

Double 9 BOOKS

# Destiny of Ukrainian Girl

**by Kishan Lal Sharma**



ISBN: 978-93-59321-07-3

**Published by**

**DOUBLE 9 BOOKS**
2/13-B, Ansari Road
Daryaganj, New Delhi – 110002
info@double9books.com
www.double9books.com
Tel. 011-40042856

# ABOUT THE AUTHOR

Kishan Lal Sharma, born on July 18, 1950, in Mehsana, Gujarat, is a multifaceted author renowned for his contributions to literature. He is the son of Smt. Chand Devi and Sri Ram Pal Sharma and is married to Indra Sharma. His educational journey includes earning a B.A. degree and a Diploma in story and screenplay writing. Sharma's literary journey began with his first work, "Rashifal," a collection of satire and taunts, published in Diwana Tej in 1978. Over the years, he has received recognition and acclaim, earning the prestigious title of Vidyavachaspati by Vikramshila Hindi Vidyapeeth, Bhagalpur in 2014 for his contributions to teaching. His writing spans across diverse genres, including stories, articles, poetry, novels, and short stories (Laghukathya), as well as reviews. Sharma's work has found a home in esteemed publications like Amar Ujala, Rajasthan Patrika, Ajit Samachar, and many more, with a consistent presence since 1978. Among his notable publications, his novel "Hara Hua Aadmi" stands out, showcasing his storytelling prowess. Additionally, his works have been featured in numerous collections, such as Laghukatha Sansar, Andhaimod, and Bharat Nepal Laghuratha Darpan, to name just a few. Kishan Lal Sharma's literary journey is a testament to his dedication and versatility as an author, and his contributions continue to enrich the world of literature with his insightful and thought-provoking writings.

# CONTENTS

# About the Novel

Anichka . . .

A girl from Ukraine.

After the Russian attack, Ukrainian citizens began to flee their country to save there lives. Anichka also had to flee the country with her mother. Her mother died in a Russian air raid before she could reach Poland to take refuge.

Like other Ukrainian refugees, she also thought that the war would end soon and she would return to her country. But seeing the war prolonging, she began to worry about her future. She had no one in this world except her mother. What will she do after returning to her country.

After a lot of thinking, she decided to leave Poland. In search of her future, she reached England via Germany and France. Here she started working in a mall. One day a customer told her.

"You look like a hollywood heroine".

"You make jokes".

"I'm not kidding . . . The young man sad, "Why are you wasting your future in the clothed shop ?"

"What to do then ?"

"Go to America. Try your luck in hollywood". The young man had awakened in her heart the dream of becoming a heroine. She came to America to fulfill that dream.

Arthur made her a heroine in his film after stumbling door to door. Her first film itself become a super hit and she became Hollywood number one heroine.

Alongwith films, marriage offer also started coming to her. Whenever some one proposes to her, she remembers her mother's past and she refuses to marry.

But she was very impressed with Johnson. So she could not refused him. But after a few days of marriage, the real face of her husband came in front of her.

Hearing the exploits of her husband, she became disgusted with her husband. She wanted to divorce her husband. But before that she wanted to answer him in her own language.

Did Anichka reply to her husband in the same language. And what happened so that Ukrainian girl. Read in the novel.

The plot of the novel, the names of the characters and the place names and events are fictitious. Matching them with any person is just a coincidence.

Thanks the Google, I got a lot of information.

How did you like the novel. Waiting for your feedback, comments and suggestions.

Kishan Lal Sharma

# I

"Why are you looking at my photo, I am in front of you".

Anuj was looking at the photo kept on his table. Then he heard a voice. He turned his head and saw.

"Hey You", Anuj didn't realize whose photo he was looking at when she came and stood in front of him. He was surprised to see Anichka in front of him. He suddenly could not believe that she was Anichka, "Am I dreaming." "This is not a dream, " said Anichka touching Anuj.

Anichka was a Hollywood superstar. Her film was being shot for the first time in Mumbai. Anuj liked Anichka. He was crazy about her acting. He was her fan, when he come to know about the shooting, he went to see the shooting. He had seen Anichka in films. But at the time of shooting he got a chance to see Anichka face to face. Even while watching the shooting, he did not even dream that Anichka could come to him one day. Thousands of people had gone to see the shooting. She could not even see him in such a crowd. Both of them did not even know each other. Then how did she reach him ? Why did she reach ?

Seeing Anichka near him, many questions arose in Anuj's mind.

"I want to talk to you"?

"From me" ? Anuj said with surprised after listening to Anichka, "Want to talk to me " ?

"Yes, From you."

"We don't even know each other."

"You are telling the truth. We do not know each other nor have we met before today."

"Then how did you reach me" ?

"Where there's a will there's a way." Anichka told how she reached him."

"But why have you come to me" ?

"Just told, I want to talk to you" ?

"Then you would have called me. I would come to you."

"I know You would have come to me." Anichka said, "But I have to talk to you. That's why I thought it appropriate."

"Tell me, what do you want to talk to me" ?

"Here in the office ? Anichka said. "Can't we sit alone somewhere else and talk" ?

"Why not" ? After listening to Anichka, Anuj said. "Let's."

Anuj came to a restaurant with Anichka. The restaurant was crowded. But one cabin was empty.

"Here we can talk" ? Anuj said while sitting.

"Sure".

Before Anichka could say anything, the waiter come with two glasses and a jug of water.

"Take it back", Anuj said. "Bring two bisleri"

"Now tell me. Why have you come to me" ?

Anuj spoke after the waiter left.

"I want to live in relationship with you." Anichka had said her point in plain words without lying any role.

"You joke well." After listening to Anichka Anuj said.

"It's not a joke."

"If not a joke then what else", Anuj said, "Hollywood's top heroine wants to live in a live-in with a humble servent working in a company, If this is not a joke then what else is ? "

"I have not come to you to joke", Anichka said seriously repeating her words, "I am serious. I want to live with you."

The waiter brought two bisleri.

"Two coffees."

The waiter took the order.

"Drink water."

Anichka opened the bottle and started drinking water.

Anuj kept watching her. After drinking water she said, "Do you accept my offer" ?

"Where are you and where is I ? Have you ever seen a king and a poor living together ? Can those living in bungalows live with those living in huts " ? Anuj had given many arguments.

"You belong the country where Lord Krishna was born. Yet you are talking like this. Even after becoming king, shri Krishna did not forget his poor friend Sudama", said Anichka, "Nothing is impossible. Everything is possible".

"But why do you want to be with a simple man like me instead of being a man of your level" ?

"The thought of being with you came to my mind on the day of the shoot.

And the scene of that day came true before her eyes.

"Where are you going" ?

Thousands of people had come to watch the sooting of the Hollywood film. Tight security arrangments were there. When Anuj broke the police cordon and started moving forward a police man caught hold of his coller.

"I want to meet the heroine. I want to get her autograph".

"No you can't go ahead".

"I will go".

Even when the policeman stopped him, he tried to move forward, then the policeman pulled him back and showed him the baton, " If you don't agree, I will beat you"

"Hit", said Anuj, "beat".

Anuj's flirtation with the policeman had attracted the attention of Anichka standing on the set. That scene had made a deep impression on Anichka's mind. She began to think. She had such a fan abroad even across the seven seas. Was also ready to get beaten up. And seeing the scene, she thought in her mind that the man she was looking for to teach her husband a lesson. He had found him.

And seeing Anuj's passion for her today in the office. She was convinced that her choice was not wrong.

"Sorry", After hearing Anichka's proposal, Anuj said, "I can not live with you".

"Why", Looking at Anuj, Anichka said, "Don't you like me" ?

"I like you. I am crazy about your beauty and acting. I like you very much. And after meeting you. I am more crazy about you".

"When you want me. You like me. You are crazy about me. Then why don't you want to be with me ?"

"You are such a big star whoever you ask to be with you. He will not live without being proud of his luck", Anuj said, "But I can't be with you".

"Coffee".

The waiter left.

"Have Coffee".

"Why can't you stay with me, "Anichka said holding the cup of Coffee in her hand.

"Because I'm married".

"So what happened? "Anichka said while taking a sip of Coffee, "I am also married".

"What? you are also married", Anuj extended his hand towards the cup and looked at Anichka with incredulous eyes.

"Yes I am also married". Anichka spoke with emphasis on each word.

"There's a difference between us getting married and you getting married". Anuj said after knowing about Anichka's marriage.

"What's the difference between being married?" Anichka said while drinking Coffee.

"Marriage is a sacred bond in our country. After getting married, husband and wife remain devoted to each other for life and remain bound in a thread", Anuj said while drinking Coffee, "Whereas in the west marriage is a contract, Stay together until you agree. If you don't agree, break the contract and hold the hand of the other".

"I have not broken the contract, nor am I asking you to separate from your wife".

"Then?" Anuj looked at Anichka with questioning eyes.

Anichka put her cup of Coffee on the table and looked out of the cabin. People were coming and going in the restaurant. It was noisy in the hall outside but inside the cabin was quiet.

"I want to live with you only for six moths. After six months you return to your country back to your wife".

"You are also married. Then why do you want to live in a live in with a stranger?" Anuj asked a question after listening to Anichka.

"My husband is living with another woman. I want to teach my husband a lesson by replying in his own language. "Anichka told the reason for living in.

"Teach your husband a lesson as you wish, "After knowing the reason of staying in live in with Anichka, Anuj said, "I cannot help you in this matter.

"If you feel that by doing this you will be unfaithful to your wife, then I will talk to your wife".

"No use", said Anuj, "Neerja will never accept your proposal".

"Have you read the Gita?"

"Why".

"Shri krishna has said in Gita, One should do one's work without worrying about the result", said Anichka, "What is your home address?"

"Why?"

"I want to meet your wife".

"Parel.................Anuj said giving the address, "I am saying once again. There is no use in going to my wife".

Anichka ignored Anuj's words. She left the restaurant and sat in the car and spoke to the driver", Parel...........

The driver set the location mentioned by Anichka in the mobile and the car started moving.

Anichka had come to Mumbai for the first time. Highrise buildings on both sides and people galloping on the roads. No one had time to look back. The car was moving forward. But the pages of her past started fluttering in front of the eyes of Anichka sitting in the car.

# II

"Mom, now the city is becoming empty. We should also go now", Anichka told mother again today.

"Wherever you want to go. You go, "Ivana said getting angry after listening to her daughter, I will not leave my house and go anywhere?"

Relations between Russia and Ukraine were normal. The dispute arose when the president of Ukraine Volodymyr Zelensky, annonced the membership of NATO.

This declaration of Ukraine provoked Russia. Ukraine's joing NATO meant. Deployment of US led NATO troops in Ukraine. Russia did not want its rival and anti US Coalition forces in its neighboring country be posted.

The deployment of NATO forces in Ukraine meant. Threat to the security of Russia. To prevent Ukraine from joining NATO, Russia attacked Ukraine.

Russian airplanes started bombing Ukraine. Missiles were fired. Russian army entered inside Ukraine. Ukrainian army set up barriers to prevent Russian army from advancing. Bridges were blownup. Mines were laid in the ground. Petrol was poured on the roads.

The cities of Luhansk, Kharkiv, Mariopol, Lviv etc were in the target of the Russian army.

The Russian army was doing most of the attacks on Mariopol, Kharkiv and Lviv. By firing bombs and missiles, Russia had destroyed Ukraine's airstrips, military bases and other defense institutions. Due to the Russian attack, not only the military bases but also the residential areas were becoming ruins.

Mariopol was a beautiful city. It used to be busy all the times. The city was becoming desolate. Most of the people had left the city to save their lives. The survivors were also slowly migrating.

Due to the air strikes, people could not even sleep properly at night. Whenever the Siren started ringing in the night. People had to run and take shelter in the bunkers. As long as the bombs and missiles kept raining on the city, people used to hide in the bunkers.

Life was worse than death. The shadow of death hovers over people's heads all the time. People had left the city to avoid death. Those who survived were also going slowly.

Anichka also wanted to leave the country and the city with her mother. She loved her city and country. She didn't want to leave here. But in the present situation it meant staying here. Embracing death or giving hands to death.

She didn't want to risk her life knowingly. That's why she wanted to leave the city. But she couldn't. She loved her mother very much. Mother was everything to her. Mother had told her. You go But she could not leave mother alone. Mother was dearer to her than her own life. And mother was not ready to leave the house.

"Get up mom............wake up mom..............

"What is it. Let me sleep". Ivana was babbling in her sleep.

Anichka was woken up by the sound of the siren. Her mother was fast asleep. When mother did not wake up even after calling repeatedly. Anichka held mother's hand and said, "Mom get up, the siren is ringing".

"Let it ring................What shall I do?" Ivana spoke in her sleep.

"Mom is about to attack".

"Bomb........... Missiles".

Then the sound of flying planes was heard in the sky. The sound of a bomb blast was also heard. Ivana get up in a panic. Holding Anichka's hand, she said, "Come on daugher........walk fast".

Bombs were falling from the sky. Anichka and Ivana ran towards the bunker. Other people also come out of the houses and ran towards the bunker.

A bomb had fallen at some distance from Ivana when the bomb exploded a piece of it jumped towards Ivana. Past her the bomb exploded, a piece of it jumped towards Ivana.

Seeing mother falling on the ground. Anichka ran towards her . . .

"Mom you are right?"

"Daughter, narrowly escaped".

"Mom hurry up..

They came inside the bunker. There were already a lot of people. That night was terrible and scary. The bombardment continued throughout the night.

There was no resistance from the Ukrainian army. How could it have happened? The Russian Airforce had already destroyed the airport, military base and other defense institutions by attacking. The communication system had been destroyed. So that no information could be sent anywhere. Bombs were being dropped so powerful that everything would be destroyed wherever it fell.

Some bombs were falling so close to the bunker that the peole sitting inside were in panic. It was dark inside the bunker. No one could see each other's face. But the fear inside could be felt in their voices.

That night the bombardment didn't stop even for a minute. Bombs were exploding outside the bunker. But the sound of the bombs bursting was so frightening that one said, "God let this night pass". The other one spoke, "Don't know whether the above one is listening or not?"

The third spoke, Let it be morning. I will leave from here.

Everyone was talking like this As the night passed by. Dawn knocked. For a long time neither the sound of the airplane nor the explosion of the bomb was heard. Then a man spoke, "It seems that there will be no more bombing". "Let's see for a while". The other man said.

And after some time people were convinced that there would be no more bombing. Then people started coming out of the bunker one by one.

"Come on daughter . . ." Ivana go with Anichka.

Mariopol had already been destroyed. What was left was ruined by the night bombardment. The marks of which were visible all around.

My house . . .

From a distance, Ivana gazed at her home. Like the other houses, his house too was reduced to rubble. Ivana ran like a madman.

My house . . . , my wardrobe . . ., my bed . . . Ivana started searching for her belonging in the pile of rubble. If the house was not left then where would the stuff be left. That too had turned to ashes.

The house was built by mother with so much effort. Ivana began to remember crying.

Ivana was raised by her mother Alice, after her father's death. Alice was a waiter in a hotel. She lived in a rented house. She had to change the rented house frequently. She was upset by this. She some how managed to buy a small plot of land. Then after working hard day and night, earned money and got the house built. Ivana had decorated that house.

The house with which her mother's memories were attached. That house was reduced to rubble by enemy bombing.

Ivana sat in the wreckage of the house crying hungry and thirsty.

"Mother, what is the use of crying. Crying will not make it back." Anichka continued to explain to her mother. But Ivana was not affected by her daughter's words. She did not move from there and the day passed. And its night.

"Mom it's been a whole day. Come on now . . .

At night, the environment started getting cold. But her mother was not ready to get up even after repeated requests. Then Anichka forcefully dragged her mother to the bunker. There were very few people inside the bunker tonight.

"Tomorrow I will also leave from here." A man said.

"Will have to go. There is nothing left to live and eat". Another man said, "How can be stay here without food and house."

That night neither the sound of an airplane nor the explosion of bombs was heard. Still people were in panic. Every one was talking among themselves. Every one talked about the same thing. Escape the city. Why don't they ? Not only the houses of the people were destroyed by the Russian air raids. The means of livelihood were also destroyed.

Anichka was listening to the people. Every one was telling to the story of the destruction of their house. After listening to those people, Anichka was also thinking in her mind.

That night neither an airplane came nor a siren sounded. The night slowly moved on.

In the morning, people started coming out of the bunker one by one.

"Come on Mom", Anichka also came out with her mother.

"Mom where are you going over there" ? Seeing Mom's foot steps, Anichka interrupted.

"Home".

"Which house" ? After listening to mother's word Anichka said laughing like a squid, "You are calling that debris home" ?

That house is a symbol of my mother. I will clean up the debris and build a house again.

Anichka was talking to her mother, then the official jeep came out announcing :

Russians attack can happen at any time. Those who are still left in the city should leave the city and go to a safe place.

"Mother, you have heard ? Now even the government is asking to leave the city".

"But daughter our house . . .

"Mom, when the war is over, we will return to our city and make our home again".

"Daughter you are telling the truth" ?

"Yes my dear mother", said Anichka hugging her mother. "We must leave the city now".

"Daughter you are sensible. Do as you see fit".

On her daughter's persuasion Ivana agreed to leave the city.

# III

"Mom you sit here".

"Where are you going" ?

"Mom I have no hope that any means will be found", Anichka said to her mother. "Still I will go around the city and came back. May be some means will be found".

Anichka sets out in search of means. The railway station and bus station had already been destroyed by Russian bombing. The only hope was private transport. She started moving forward in search of a car or taxi. The city which was buzzing earlier. There were tall buildings, offices of companies, market and malls. Where there used to be crowd all the time. People were seen laughing. There was silence like crematorium in that city. High rise buildings, mall, markets were all turned into rubble. The Russian bombardment turned the city into a crematorium.

Anichka was not as distressed as seeing the city turned into a pile of debris. She was more saddened to see the dead bodies lying on the piles of debris. There was no one to lift those dead bodies, to perform their last rites. Don't know how long these dead bodies will remain unclaimed. Will has last rites be performed or will his body just rot away.

Earlier, she used to feel cheerful while passing through the city. Today, seeing the plight of the same city, looked sad and extinguished.

She walked a long distance on foot. Nothing was visible except silence, heaps of debris and sign of destruction. Seeing the condition of the city, she realized that there is no use in going further. There is no possibility of getting any means. She thought it better to return than to go ahead.

"What happened daughter" ? asked Ivana, looking at Anichka.

"There is nothing left of the city except heaps of corpses and heaps of rubble".

"So what will happen now" ? After listening to the daughter, Ivana said.

"Will have to walk" ?

"Where to walk" ?

"Poland", Anichka said, "The refugee camp is there".

"On foot . . . Poland . . . you have gone mad". Ivana said after listening to her daughter. "Is this what Poland has kept more than 1300 kilometers."

"Mom, I am not talking about walking to Poland".

"Then".

"Mom, I am not talking about walking from here", said Anichka, "If we go further, we will definitely found some means".

"If you don't get here, how will you get it when you go ahead" ?

"Mom Russian's attack are not happening on all the cities right now. Most of them are happening on Mariopol, Kharkiv. Luiv and Lahansak etc. Anichka explain to mom.

"Come on, when no means is found, we will have to walk on foot", Ivana got up and said, "Let's see what happens next".

And Ivana walked on foot with her daughter. Debris was scaltened all around and mutilated dead bodies were lying every where. Ivana's soul screamd after seeing that terrible scene.

"What a butcher Putin. What is he getting by killing innocent people".

Anichka knew her mother hates Russia. That's why she was abusing Russian and cursing Putin.

Anichka and Ivana came far away from Mariupol. Then they were joined by other people. Ivana said to a woman, "You too are leaving the country".

"What to do ? Have to go" ?

As they started moving forward, the number of people started increasing. And by the time they reached Zavodske there was a group of fifty people.

There were women, men and children of all ages in that group. They were tired of walking, so they stopped for a while to rest.

They were all from the same country and the same city. But all unknown to each other and unfamiliar. But the pain was the same for all. Their city and home were destroyed. There was no source of livelihood left. These people were displaced from their country and were going to take refuge in the neighboring country.

"Oh look at that". One of the man in the convoy said while gesturing".

And the eyes of the people of the convoy went in the direction of that man's hand. A bus was standing in the distance. The old man again said. "Talk to him. May be he will ready to go" ?

"You guys stayed here". A young man said, "I will come after talking".

"I will also go with you". The another youngman said

"That would be fine". The other middle aged man said.

And the two young men went to talk to the bus driver. The bus was empty. The driver of the bus was nowhere to be seen. Seeing the bus empty the first young man said, Where is the driver ?

"Come on. Let's find the driver". After listening to the first young man, the second young man said.

"Where" ? The first young man said, "If the bus is standing here, he will come here. This is we wait for" .

"You are right",

And both those young men stood there waiting for the driver. After some time a man came humming .

"You are the driver of the bus" ?

"Yes". He said, "Why".

"We have to go", the first young man said. "Will you go" ?

"Where" ?

"Medyka".

"It is on the Poland border".

"Yes, we have to go there" . Both the young men spoke together.

"Take a taxi", Driver said, "You will definitely get a taxi if you go further".

"Why taxi" ? The first young man said.

"If you two go by bus, then the bus will be very expensive. A taxi would be cheaper for you".

"we are not two", Another young man gestured with his hand, "We are fifty. The rest of the people are sitting there".

"Now I understand. Russians has destroyed our country. Not only Mariopol, Lviv, Kharkiv, Luhausk now the whole of Ukraine is in the grip of Russia's attack". He said. "You are going to seak asylum in Poland".

"What to do ? We did't want to leave the country. But we have to go. Now even our government has told to go to a safe place".

"I will take you. But I will take a ride for twenty thousands rupees".

"That's four times", said another young man, "One we have to be homeless from our country. And instead of helping you are taking advantage of the helplessness".

"What to do ? I am also helpless. Most of the petrol pumps have been destroyed. Those who are left are giving petrol at twice or thrice the price. Then I will also have to come back with an empty bus".

No matter what the disaster is. Be it natural or manmade. Some people find opportunities even in disaster, Corona was a global pandemic. No Country remained untouched by the outbreak of this pandemic. It was such a disease that anyone could fall prey to. Still some people took advantage of this epidemic. Earned a lot of money by black marketing, hoarding. Man was no longer a man, he become a vulture. The country was not even completly free from Corona that Russia attacked.

Not only military bases, government institutions and factories were being destroyed by the war. People private property was also being destroyed. Not only Ukrainian soldiers but also common people were being killed in the Russian attack. There were children among those who died. Even such small children who had not even taken care of their senses Dead bodies were lying unclaimed everywhere. There was no one to perform their rituals.

On the one hand people were troubled by the war. Homes were destroyed and means of employment were also destroyed. So they were forced to migrate. On the other hand there was no dearth of profit makers amidst the fury of the war. Would have done anything out of desperation. Both the young men knew that the bus driver was asking for more money. But if you want to save your life you will have to give it. Money is dirty. If we stay alive then we will earn.

"I can't take a decision alone. People with me are sitting in front", Said the first young man, "I will talk to them and tell".

"Yes do it", Bus driver said, "But quickly".

Both the young men returned. When they told about the fare, a man said. "It is too much".

"Uncle I also know, it is more. But in this condition It is difficult to get any means. There is a problem of petrol. And whoever goes has to come back as well".

"You are right". An old man supported the young man.

The fare was high. Everyone was arguing with each other. Whether to go or not. An opinion could not be formed among them. Then the voice of the bus driver was heard, "If you want to go, came quickly. Otherwise I am leaving" "We are coming", Said an old man after listening to the bus driver, "If this one is gone then it is difficult to find another means".

That old man walked towards the bus. Some people followed him with heart and some people reluctantly. That old man went to the bus driver and said, "You are demanding for more fare".

"Uncle what should I do, Getting petrol is very difficult and also expensive".

"Son we are all upset. Everyone's house has been destroyed and now we have to leave our country too.......... After a lot of persuasion by the old man driver agreed to take three thousands rupees less per ride.

One by one people started walking towards the bus. But an old woman remained sitting on the ground.

"What happened grandmother?" A young man came to her and said, "Why did you sit down".

"You go son".

"You will not go?"

"No son. I will not go".

"Grandmother here life is in danger?"

"Son, now life is of how many days? I have already lost my husband and son in the war. Now why run away leaving the country for a little life".

"Grandma, If life was not dear to you, You would not have left your city and ran away", That young man said, "Tell me why you are not going? If you do not tell me, I will not go either".

When the young man repeatedly asked, the old woman hesitantly said, "I have less money".

"That's all. Don't worry. Consider me your son. "The young man took the old woman's hand and took her to the bus.

"Everyone has come? Said the driver", Is there anyone left?"

"No".

"Then go?"

"Yes".

Several voices were heard at once and the bus started.It would take at least twenty hours to reach the border of Poland Petrol was needed for such a long journey. The driver started the bus and said, "First of all Petrol has to be taken".

"Is there no Petrol in the bus?" A woman had asked.

"There is Petrol", The driver said, "But our journey is long. Petrol will have to be taken from many places."

The driver was also looking both sides while driving the bus. Many petrol pumps. Came on the way but they were closed. When the bus reached. Dinparo, a petrol pump was seen open.

"Petrol is?" The driver asked while parking the bus at the petrol pump.

"Will get", The petrol pump by said, "One hundred fifty Hayvnia litre".

"That's more than double".

"Petrol is available in such circumstances what is the less". The bus driver started arguing with the petrol pump boy.

"Why are you arguing with me ? I am a servant", said the petrol pump boy. "If you find it expensive then don't take it".

"Have to take".

"How much?"

"Fill up the petrol tank".

After filling petrol in the bus, the bus started. After running some distance, the bus stopped. The driver got down from the bus and said, "You people should eat and drink here. It is not known whether any hotel will be open or not in the way".

One by one people started getting off the bus. Anichka said to her mother, "Come on, Let us also eat something".

"No daughter. I am not hungry". Ivana said. "you go and eat'.

"Mom, you haven't eaten anything since yesterday". Said Anichka, "If you don't eat, I won't either".

She could not stand the stubbornness of her daughter. She had to get down from the bus with her daughter.

After half an hour the bus started again. The people sitting in the bus belonged to the same country. But they had come from different places. That's why they were unfamiliar with each other. After the bus started, they started introducing themselves to each other. After some time they got acquainted with each other.

After being introduced, they started sharing each others sorrows. Anichka was talking to the people sitting in the bus. But Ivana was silent.

After running for several hours, the bus stopped at Zaporiz Zhia.

Seeing the petrol pump open here, the driver got petrol filled in the bus. The passenger had tea and breakfast. After some time the bus started again. There was very less traffic on the road. The driver was driving the bus fast. It was night by the time the bus reached Ternopil.

As soon as the night fell, people began to fear airstrikes. Till now most of the attacks were happening on the cities bordering Russia. But other cities were also not untouched by air strikes. Russian attacks had also taken place on the cities bordering Poland.

People were talking to each other during the day. But as soon as night fell, silence spread in the bus. People were praying to God in their hearts that there should be no air raids in the night and they would reach Poland safely. And the bus reached Lviv. Here the driver got petrol refilled in the bus. People also had food.

The night was slowly slipping away. There was no noise except the sound of the bus running. The bus was running at a high speed. The last hour of the night had began. There were only a few hours left for the dawn the begin.

'What happened" ? After some time the bus suddenly stopped while moving. Olek asked.

"I see. Said the driver as he got down from the bus. Fedir and Olek also got down from the bus.

"There is some fault in the bus". After some time the driver said. "From here you will have to go on foot".

"On foot", Olek spoke, after listening to the driver, "why" ?

"No mechanic will be available at this time. I will look for a mechanic in the morning". The driver told the problem.

"How far is the boarder from here" ? Fedir asked.

"About five kilometers".

What would people do ? There was no other way. One by one people got off the bus and started walking. Anichka with her mother got off the bus last ? A group of fifty people started walking in a long queue. Anichka was at the back with mother.

After Russia attacked Ukraine, the USA and EU countries imposed economic sanction on Russia Ukrain's defence institutions and war materials were destroyed by Russia's attack. USA and EU countries provided financial assistance to Ukraine along with supply of military equipment, All aid was coming to Ukraine through Poland.

Russia was shocked by this. He had warned Poland that if weapons came through it to Ukraine, he would attack Poland as well.

Happiness was slowly returning to the faces of the people moving towards the border of Poland. As the border of Poland was coming closer, there faces were glowing with happiness. In Ukraine, they were living every moment under the shadow of death. The fear of death will not however over their heads every moment in the refugee camp.

Suddenly airplanes started hovering in the sky. Seeing the shadow of death hovering over their heads, people who were walking in a line earlier started running here and there. Anichka and Ivana also ran. Anichka was young while her mother was old. Airplanes hovering in the sky began to bomb. Anichka and Ivana were also running to avoid the bomb hit.

While running Anichka went ahead and Ivana remained behind. Then a bomb fell near Ivana. As soon as the bomb exploded, Ivana body was torn in pieces.

"Mom...Mom..." Anichka ran away screaming.

"Mom...Mom..." Anichka started crying while sitting on the ground. While moaning she was mumbling, "Mom, you didn't want to come. I brought you forcefully if I have not brought, you would have been alive".

Fearing death, Anichka had brought her mother. That death had also come with Ivana. Anichka was crying. Bombs were raining continuously from the sky. Everyone was worried about his life. In such a situation who would pay attention to Anichka's cry.

Fade, the one who had come for ahead. Seeing Anichka crying, ran to her. Holding Anichka's hand said. "Come on daughter. Airplanes are raining bombs".

"Mom... my mother...".

"Where is your mother now ? She had left this world. She will not come back because of your crying". Fade explaining to Anichka said, "Daughter accept the truth. Your mother's body has bean broken into so many pieces that you would not even be able to collect them.

Anichka did not want to get up but. Fade took her hand and brought her with him.

"Mom...Mom..."

Anichka was crying and lookind back. Fade brought her to the border of Poland.

# IV

Ukraine is bordered by Russia to the east Balarus, Poland and Slovakia to the north, Hungry to the west and Romania and Maldons to the sounth west.

After Russia's attack on Ukraine, Ukrainian citizens started fleeing from their country to save their lives. Poland opposed Russia's attack on Ukraine. Many other countries did not want war between Russia and Ukraine. But war could not be stopped. Poland had opened the border of its country for refugees coming from Ukraine, showing humanity.

Refugees from war torn Ukraine were being warmly welcomed in Poland. All the refugees who came to Poland hopes that the war would end soon and they would return to their contry.

Citizens of Poland were coming forward to help the refugees from Ukraine, Some were giving clothes, Some were giving food or medicines.

Every citizen of Poland was helping according to their ability. Many people had opened doors of their homes to the refugees.

Anna came again today to deliver food to the refugee camp. She reached out to the Anichka while distributing food packets. Anichka was sitting sad and lost.

"Take this".

"I do not want". Anichka refused to take the food packet.

"You will not eat food?" Anna said on Anichka's refusal, "Yesterday you did not take?"

"She hasn't eaten or drink anything. Since yesterday". Sitting beside Anichka, said Maria, "She had been sitting like this since yesterday".

"What is your name?" Anna asked her.

"Anichka".

"Who else is with you?"

Anichka started crying on hearing Anna's words.

"What happened ? Why are you crying?" Seeing Anichka crying, Anna said.

"Her mother". Maria spoke.

"What happened to her mother". Anna looked at Maria.

"Her mother...some distance away from the border..." Angelina had told about the death of Anichka's mother in the bombing.

"My mother did not want to leave the country. I had brought her forcefully. If I had not brought her. She would have been alive". Anichka started crying again rembering her mother.

"Anichka don't cry" Anna sitting beside Anichka conscled her and said, "It is not your fault. It was God's will".

Anna sat beside Anichka and explained to her. After explaining for a long time, Anichka stopped crying and there was silence between them. After some time Anna broke the silence. And said,

"Will you come with me?"

"Where?" Anichka looking at Anna said. "My house".

"Your house?"

"Yes". Anna repeated again, "My house".

"Leave it. What will I do at your house? I am fine here".

"Oh come on", Anna said holding Anichka's hand.

"Leave it. You will be in trouble because of me".

"There will be no problem", Anna brought Anichka with her to her house.

"Mom...Mom..." Anna shouted as soon as she entered the house.

"Where are you Mom?" On not getting the answer, Anna again said, "Where are you Mom come here".

"What happende?" Hearing daughter's voice. Carolina came in the room and said.

"Look Mom. Who I brought with me".

"Who is she?" Carolina asked looking at the stranger who had come with her daughter.

"She is Anichka".

"Anichka", Carolina said, "Anichka who?"

Anichka is a Ukrainian refugee, "Anna spoke", There was an accident near the Polish border with Anichka".

"Accident", After listening to the daughter, Carolina said, "What kind of accident".

"Her mother... Anna, told her mother about Anichka's accident in an air raid near our country's border while coming from Ukraine.

"Whatever God wants, only happens. Everyone is helpless in front of him", Carolina, putting her hand on Anichka's back and explaning to her. "Daughter, I cannot fulfill the lack of your mother. But you consider me as your mother. Like I am Anna's mother. So is yours".

"Come with me", Anna took Anichka to her room. She opened the wardrobe and said, "Take out the clothes you like. Go to the bathroom and fresh up. Then we will sit and eat together".

"Sister you only take it out".

"Whatever you like. Take it out".

Anichka look out a pair of clothes, then she went to the bathroom.

"Anichka come quickly". Anna was waiting for Anichka at the dining table.

"Sister I don't feel like eating".

After listening to Anichka, Anna said, "Eat as much as you want".

Anna forcefully fed her.

Anna and Anichka lay on the same bed at night. Anna asked her, "What did you do there" ?

"Graduated this year".

Anna kept taking information from Anichka about her mother and her country. She wanted to mix with Anichka. So that she would not feel alienated. And forget the sorrow of losing her mother.

"What you do"? Anichka asked Anna.

"My NGO is".

Anna was a social worker. She used to run an NGO. She worked for the welfare of women and children. After Russia's attack on Ukraine, the process of refugees started coming to Poland. Many organizations of Poland were engaged in helping the refugees. Some were giving clothes, some food and some medicines.

Anna's NGO was providing food to the refugees. She started delivering food packets in a refugee camp. She had connected many people of the city to her organization. They were helping her organization physically and financially.

After watching Anna's way of working for two days, Anichka said to her, "I also want to help you in your work".

"Really"?

"Yes Anna. I want to help you with your work".

"I would be happy if you would work with me. I would have support and you would not feel bored either.

"Let us go".

And Anna took Anchika with her. Anichka started helping Anna in her work.

Anichka herself a Ukrainian refugee, began working for refugees from her country in Poland.

The car stopped a jolt. Anichka returning from the past to the present said. "What happened".

"Red Signal".

Anichka looked. The traffic at the intersection was at a standstill. She sat in the car and started looking, sometimes to the right, some times to the left and sometimes in front. Long queues of vehicles were visible everywhere.

As soon as the green signals was given, the vehicles of her side started moving. Anichka car also started running on the road again. Looking at the buildings on both sides of the road. She again got lost in her past.

# V

Anichka, like every Ukrainian was thinking that the war would end soon. And she will return to her country. The house which was built by her grandmother and her mother decorated. That house was destroyed in a Russia airstrikes. It was turned into rubble. Mom loved her house very much. Now mom was no more. She will return to her country and fulfill Mom's wish. She will rebuild that house.

Most of the countries of the world wanted, the ongoing was between Russia and Ukraine should stop. The cessation of war was very important for world peace. The heads of France, Turkey and Israel had also tried to stop the war.

The General Secetary of UNO had also appealed to stop war. India's Prime minister Modi had also said, "This is not the time for war. The solution to every issue is dialogue".

But instead of ending the war was getting more and more gruesome as it dragged on.

Russia had ruined Ukraine's military capacity in a few days by throwing its entire military power into the war. Ukraine's air bases, weapons depots and military installations were destroyed. Without arms and ammuntion the war cannot be fought. Russia was confident that Ukraine would surrender if its military capability was destroyed.

But this did not happen. The reason for this was the economic and military help given to Ukraine by NATO and European countries.

Initially, due to Russian attack the Ukrainian army seemed to be lagging behind in the war. But after getting military help, the Ukrainian army get organized and started fighting the Russian army. The war which Russia expected to win soon, the war slowly started getting prolonged.

Seeing the war not ending, the refugees from Ukraine started worrying about their future. Anichka also started thinking about her future. Earlier She was also thinking that after the end of the war, She would return to her country. But seeing the war being prolonged, there was a change in her thinking.

She started thinking as long as mother was alive, she had everything in Ukraine. What was left of her when mother was no more. If she waits for the end of the was and when the war is over, even if she returns to her country, what will be left for her there? It takes decades to rebuild a country ravaged by war. It takes only a few moments to be destryoed by war but it takes years to rebuild.

After a lot of thinking, Anichka did not see any future in returning to her country after the end of the war. So after thinking for several days, She decided to go ahead. After making up her mind one day Anichka said to Anna, "I want to leave".

"Why" Anna said in surprise after listening to Anichka, "Do you have any problem here or did I make a mistake"?

"What are you talking abot sister. You have given shelter to an unknown stranger, sad girl in your house. I got love from your mother like my own mother. I never felt that. I am living with stranger. Here I feel like I am living in my home with my own people".

"Still you want to leave from here"? After listening to Anichka's words, Anna looked at her and said.

"Sister, I want to leave here for my future". Anichka had told Anna the reason for leaving Poland after listening to her, Anna said, "you were saying that you will return to your country after the war is over" ?

"There is no sign of the end of the war", said Anichka, "Anyway who is mine in Ukraine now I had only mother, She also left me and went away. Then what I will do after going there".

"You must have thought of something", Anna said, after listening to Anichka's words.

"For the time being. I intend to go to Germany. Then it is up to fate. Where fate takes me?

"You want to go to make your future, So I will not stop you. But you have considered me as a sister, then I will definitely give advice".

"What sister"?

"The world is not what it seems. Don't trust anyone blindly. You have to be alert all the time, "Said Anna explaining like an elder sister", People keep Vulture eyes on a single woman all the time. Don't get trapped in the clutches of such people.

"Sister I will always remember your advice".

"Will you not forget me after leaving here" ?

"Do you think so" ?

"No, you fool", said Anna patting Anichka's cheek, "I was just joking".

And one day she was about to leave, then Anna gave her a thousnad dollars and said. "Keep this".

"Sister, I have money".

"Never mind keep them too". Anichka had to keep the money on Anna's insistence. While travelling from Poland to Germany by train, she was reading the history of Germany on Google. Germany played an important role in starting both world wars. Germany is incomplete without Hitler. The world has not forgotten Hitler and will not forget it even today.

Hitler was born on 20 April 1889. The First World War began after the assassination of Archduke Ferdinande, heir to the Austrohungarian Empire. More than thirty countries participated in the First World War. On one side were Germany, Austria, Hungary, Ottoman and Bulgaria.

On the other side were Britain, France, Russia, America, Japan etc. This war started on 28 June 1914.

When World War I strated, Hitler joined the German army. He participated in many battles in France. In 1918, he had to be hospitalized after being injured.

Germany was defeated in the First World War. After defeat had to sign the Treaty of Versailles on 28 June 1919.

According to this treaty, Germany had to lose a large part of the land. He could not control other countries. The size of his army was limited and a heavy indemnity was imposed on him.

Not only Hitler but other German citizens were also feeling insulted by this humiliating treaty. This treaty laid the foundation of the Second World War.

Hitler formed the Nazi party and gradually came to power in Germany. During his rule nationalism rose and the humiliating treaty of the First World War became the cause of the Second World War. This war lasted from 1939 to 1945 Germany had the upper hand in this war. But Germany's attack on Russia was its biggest mistake. Which became the reason for its defeat. Distraught by this defeat Hitler committed suicide.

After this war, Germany was divided into two parts- East and West. After fourty five years, Germany divided into two parts was united on october 3, 1990. This was the first event in world history.

Anichka fell asleep while sitting. When she opened her eyes, she found a man sitting on the front seat. When she woke up, the man smiled and said, I am Benjamin from Germany You do not look like from Germany? Where are you from"?

"Ukraine".

"Oh ho...Ukraine is in bad condition at this time", He said while cursing Russia, describing the plight of there, "Russia had divided our country into two parts. Brother had divided brother. Now Ukraine is ruined Putin is doing arbitrary and the world is watching the spectacle.

Anichka kept listening to him.

"Where are you from in Ukraine"?

"Mariupol".

"It was a very beautiful city. Russia destroyed it".

"You have seen"?

"Yes. I've been there twice". said Benjamin. "How's Germany going"?

"Looking for work".

Before reaching Berlin, he had become so attached to Anichka that he told her, "Don't worry about work. I will got you work".

On reaching Berlin, Coming out of the Statim, Benjamin said to Anichka, "Let's have tea and breakfast first".

Benjamin took Anichka to a hotel. After ordering the waiter, he said the Anichka, "I will go to the washroom".

When Benjamin left, a waiter came up to her and said, "Where are you from" ?

"Ukraine".

"Refugee", said the waiter, "You know the man with you" ?

"No", said Anichka, "I met him in the train".

"Stay away from him. He is a pimp of woman. Brings foreign woman by trapping in his trap and sells them in brothels".

The waiter was gone. She remembered what Anna had said, "The world is not what it seems. Women are in denger at every step".

Benjamin had returned from washroom. After having breakfast and tea. Came out of the hotel and said, "I will call a taxi".

"No need".

"Why" ?

"I have decided to return from here".

"Where" ?

"Where I came from".

"I will get you a job".

"I don't want to work here".

Anichka did not listen to Benjamin and returned to the station. She was thanking god in her heart. God had saved her from falling in to the mine of prostitutes.

And she left for France by train.

On her way to Paris. She was looking up the history of France on Google.

France is also a country in Europe. The history of France is glorious. And it is known for many reasons. But it can not be without the mention of Eiffel Tower and Napoleon.

Napoleon was born in a simple French family. With his bravery, ability and intelligence, he bacame the commander of the French army. He also participated in the French revolution. And later he became the emperor of France.

Nepoleon is counted among the most successful generals in history. He won every war and established a vast empire. In 1815 he attacked Russia without thinking and considering the strategy. This proved to be his biggest mistake and he had to face defeat. That defeat is remembered in history by the name of waterloo.

That defeat laid the foundation for his downfall. He had to spent the last time of his life as a prisoner on St. Helena Island.

On coming to Paris from Germany, Anichka could not stop herself and went to see the Eiffel Tower.

The Eiffel Tower is famous in the world. It is a huge iron pillar. It was built in 1889 for the world trade fair in France. It was designed by Gustave Eiffle. When it was built, it was the tallest tower in the world. Height is 324 meters.

The Eiffel Tower is built on the Seine River in Paris. It is one of the most remarkable construction in the world. It is a symbol of French culture. It is open to tourists throught the year.

"Wow". Anichka stood and looked at the Eiffel Tower for a long time.

On arrival in Paris, she started looking for work. She went from place to place in search of work. She also visited many hotels. At last she got a job as a waiteress in Cocatte restaurant. After getting the job, she said to the restaurant owner, "I don't have any place to stay right now. Can I stay here for the night".

"Yes, you may stay". Said Charles, the owner of the restaurant, "David also stay here in night.

The restaurant was open until ten at night. Anichka worked while the restaurant was open and went to sleep when the restaurant closed. She slept upstairs and David down the hall. Toilet was down stairs so she had to come down stairs at night for toilet. Being with a man she could not spend night carefree. She used to be afraid that David might misbehave with her.

Don't know what was written in Anichka's fate. She could not work in the restaurant for a long time. One day a waiter of the restaurant fell ill. His corona test was done which came positive. After getting corona patient, corona test was done for all the employees of the restaurant. Many more employees were found corona positive. The administration sealed the restaurant for a month.

When the restaurant was sealed, Anichka had no work, no place to stay. She tried to find work elsewhere. But when she could not find work, she decided to leave France.

Where to be.

After much thought she decided to go to England. And she left for England. On her way to England she was thinking about England.

England which is also known as UK or great Britain. It also includes Scotland, Wales and Northern Ireland. There was a time when England ruled the whole except some countries of the world. That's why the proverb was prevalent that -The Sun never sets in the rule of England Now this proverb has been comfined to the pages of history.

Anichka started looking for a job as soon as she came to London. After a few days of running she got a job as a salesgirl in Cardinal Mall. Two other girls with her in that shop. Men and women of all ages used to come to the shop to buy clothes. She greets every customers with a smile and her behavior and eloquence charm the customer so much that he buys something.

One day a young man came to shop.

"Hello sir", Anichka said welcoming the young man with a smile. "What can I show you" ?

"Jeans".

Anichka started showing different brands of jeans to that young man. The young man's attention was less on seeing the jeans and more on seeing her. Anichka was shocked by this act of that young man. "Are you looking at the jeans or me" ?

"To you".

"Why me". Anichka said, "Haven't you seen any girl before" ?

"Every day I see. Girls are seen as soon as I step out of the house".

"Why are you looking at me like this when you see girls every day".

"There is something special about you".

"What do you see in me" ?

"You look like a hollywood heroine".

"You make good jokes".

"I'm not kidding". The young man said.

"You are realy look like a Hollywood heroine".

"Really" ?

"Seriously, you look like a Hollywood heroine", the young man repeated his point again. "Why are you wasting your future in a clothes shop" ?

"What should I do them" ? Looking at the young man, Anichka said.

"Go to America and try your luck in Hollywood".

The young man left without buying anything. But Anichka's heart was stirred.

Is that young man telling the truth. Do I look like a heroine. Hollywood heroine. After the departure of that young man, many questions started arising in Anichka's mind. From whom should she ask the answers to these. She did not see anyone to answer the question raised in her mind. Then she decided to find the answers to these questions herself.

And she watched many hollywood movies. Back to the future, The shining. Get out, Life is beautiful etc.

Seeing the heroine of those films, she got the answer. The young man was telling the truth. She can became a heroine. A hollywood heroine. And she started seeing her future in hollywood.

Ukrainian refugees were allowed to go any where in Europe. But she could not go to America without necessary documents. She got the papers prepared in a hurry.

One more day.

Left for America to try her luck.

# VI

Anichka was studying the history of America while going there. The name of Christopher Columbus is associated with America. Columbus was a seafarer, pirate, colonial explorer. He was not the first European to reach America. He traveled to America four time, which was funded by queen Isabella of Spain. He tried to establish a sattlement there and laid the foundation of spanish colonialism in America.

Today America is a super power. The most powerfull country in the world. Leading in every field.

Can any one imagine that today's super power America would have been a slave once.

But the reality is the same. America has also been a colony of great Britain. In the year 1600 Great Britain made America its slave. There was a long struggle to overthrow the shackles of slavery. Overthrow British power in 1776.

After independence, America moved on the path of progress by forgotting the memories of slavery.

Anichka moved from London to New York. New York has the statue of liberty. It is a sculpture made of copper. Which is one hundred and fifty one feet high. Including the foundation stone, its height is three hundres and five feet. In 1886, this statue was presented by France to America.

People coming to New York, domestic and foreign, do not forget to see the statue of liberty. Anichka went to see it as soon as she landed at the airport. Anichka didn't come to America, Unnecessarily.

She come with a goal, a purpose. Anichka's goal was to become an actress. Her goal was to become a heroine. Her desire was to become a Hollywood heroine and she came to America from England with this dream in mind.

Anichka was fond of dencing. She had done small roles in plays when she was studying. She loved Shakespeare's play's.

When she was young, the idea of working in films came to her mind after watching films. But the war had buried the thought that came to her mind.

And this idea would probably remain buried in the heart. If that day the customer did not come. And that customer awakened such a feeling in her mind that she started thinking day and night about becoming a Hollywood heroine. And to implement her idea, she moved to America. Hollywood is located in the city Los Angeles in the state of California.

Anichka was thinking of Hollywood on her may to Los Angeles from New York.

Los Angeles has a member of film studios. Thomas Alva Edison invented the Kinetoscope. Some of the film industry has shifted from Los Angeles to Barbac and west the side. Still most of the films are made here.

Movies are a cheap means of entertainment. Rich or poor, man or woman, young or old. People of all age groups watch movies. Earlier one had to go to the cinema hall to watch movies. Now there are many means like home theatre, computer, mobile, TV etc are available through which the film can be seen at home or anywhere.

Hollywood films have their own craze. Hollywood films are liked all over the world because of their excellent technique, excellent filming, superb acting and editing. There are fans of Hollywood Fimls in every country.

Films are shot indoor as well as outdoor. In 1911, the Nestor company opened the first studio named old Tavern. It was a suitable location for the studio because of the open sky, attractive natural scenery and hills.

The echo of 'Me-too', was heard in the past.

It is a social movement. Started against sexual harassment and sexual assault. In this, woman tell about sexual harassment and sexual offenses against them.

The term 'me too', was first used by sexual harassment activist 'Tarana Burke".

The purpose of this movement was to express sympathy towards the sexually harassed people and raise their voice unitedly against it. Empowering women in particular. In 2018, that movement spread rapidly after allegations of sexual harrasment against 'Harvey Weinstein'.

The effect of this movement in Hollywood was that many high ranking people had to resign or were relieved of their service. Started on Twitter, the 'hashtag me too', became the 'person of the year', in the famous magazine Times'.

Hollywood may not have been untouched by 'me-too', But the desire to make a career in films has not ended among young women. Whether it is a young man or a young woman, everyone wants to become a star. The main reason for this is wealth and fame. To appear on the film screen means to capture the hearts of the people. Anichka also came to Los Angeles with the dream of becoming a heroine. By becoming a heroine, She wanted to add her name in the list of famous heroined like Scarlett, Jennifer Lawrence, Anne Hathaway, Angelina Jolle. She wanted to rule the hearts of people by becoming a heroine.

But it was not an easy task. It could be done as she wanted, when a producer gave her the role of heroine in his film.

Undoubtedly, she was the owner of youth. She was the owner of beautiful body. She was no less than an apsara in beauty. She had all the qualities to be a heroine in her own eyes.

She first met producer Robert to get a role in the film and Robert told her, "sorry, I have signed the heroine" for my next film. Anyway, I don't bet on the new girl".

Anichka started hopping from one studio to another. But she did not get work from any producers. But she neither gave up nor was disappointed. After meeting several producer, she met producer Jansan. He said, "First you have to screen test".

Jansan had called Anichka to the hotel fo the screen test. In that hotel, a room was permanently booked in Jansan's name. Anichka had reached for the screen test.

"Stand in front of the Camera".

Anichka stood up.

"Turn right".

"Turn around".

"Smile".

"Put your hand on your cheek".

Jansan took several photographs of Anichka in various poses.

"Skirt up".

Anichka hesitated after listening to Jansan.

"Skirt up". Jansan spoke again.

Anichka hesitatingly after raising the skirt of Anichka, he took different poses. Then he said, "Take of your clothes".

"What do you mean"? After listening to Jansan, Anichka started looking at him with questining eyes.

"You don't understand meaning of stripping". Jansan said, "get naked and stand in front of the Camera.

"Why"? said Anichka, "What is the need of it"?

"I am the director or you"?

"You".

"So I say do it".

"What"?

"Take off all your clothes".

"Sorry".

"Sorry will not work. I have nude scene in my film. If you want to work in my film then you have to be nude".

"Sorry. I will not do that". Anichka did not take a moment to come out of the hotel room.

Anichka had heard that wherever the film industry is, girls are exploited. Girls make compromises to work in films.

Earlier, these things used to come out in a filter. But when the, "me-too", movement started, the woman who had been victims of sexual abuse gathered courage, And shared the story and pain of sexual abuse with people on social media.

Anichka's dream of going to the film world was not broken even after listening to the plight of the victimized women through, "me-too".

Anichka did not want to take shortcuts to get work in films. She had full faith in her beauty, ability and talent. But her beauty, ability,talent was not working.

Some producers were ready to give her work, but wanted to make her a bed before signing her in their film. Some producer had said this thing in a roundabout way, while some had said it in clear words.

The "Me-Too", movement was not over yet. Due to this movement many peole had to lose their position, respect and social prestige. Still people were not deterred. The female body has beeb treated as a commodity. Goods are sold in market culture.

Even today, there is no dearth of such women in the society, who do not refrain from adopting the shortcut path to earn wealth and fame. This path goes through the body of the woman. They are ready to do anything to get work in the film.

Wherever she went, she was disappointed. But she did not get discouraged. She kept hopping from one studio to another seeing her wandering in search of work, many brokers also followed her. But she did not fall for the touts. She wanted to work in the film. But on her own.

One day she was coming out of a studio. Then she encountered a young man.

"You want to be a heroine"?

"Yes", Anichka said, "How did you know"?

"Very simple", The young man said, "Young men and women come here with the dream of working in films".

"But who are you"? Anichka said after listening to that young man.

"My name is Arthur", said Arthur, introducing himself, "I was Jansan's assistant".

"Was", said Anichka, "listening to Arthur, "Means"?

"I mean I left him".

"Left such a big producer and director. "Why"?

"During the shooting of a scene in the film, there was a dipute with Jansan".

"I will make my film", Arthur said", You are asking about me only. Will you tell something about yourself also".

"I'm Anichka, a Ukrainian refugee". She told her story of coming to America from Ukraine.

"You have come here with the dream of working in films".

"Yes". Anichka nodded

"Wandering from door to door but still haven't found work".

"No".

"Don't worry. I will make you a heroine", Arthur said, "You will be heroine of my film".

Anichka had come to America only to become a heroine. After wandering from door to door, far from becoming a heroine, no producer was even ready to give a small role in his film.

That's why she immediately accepted Arthur's proposal.

# VII

"What is the title of the film"? Anichka had asked Arthur.

"Live in relation with celebatory".

"The title of the film is new and interesting".

"The story is as interesting as the title".

"Who is the writer"?

"I".

"You are the producer, director as well as the story writer".

"Yes". And Arthur narrated the story of the film to Anichka.

"Interseting". Anichka said after listening to the story.

"The heroine has been found for the film. Now the rest of the actors have to be selected".

Arthur started selecting the actors for his film. Along with the hero-heroine, the rest of the actors of the film were also newly selected. There were two reasons for this. Old actors ask for more money, due to which the budget of the film increased. And shooting with older actors also comes with date issues. Due to which there is delay in the completion of the film and the the budget of the film also increases.

Arthur got the songs for the film written by Veteran lyricist Harry but chose young composer Boston to compose the music.

The story of the film was written by Arthur himself but the screenplay and dialogues were written by Neil.

The cameramen and technicians were old and experienced people for the film.

Now the problems was to find a studio for indoor shooting of the film.

There are hundreds of studios in Los Angeles. Arthur started circling from one studio to another. But no studio was vacant studio are booked one or two years in advance for shooting. Arthur used to search for vacant studio. One day he reached Paramount studio. He was familiar with th owner of the studio, Robin. On seeing him Robin said, "How are you"?

"Fine".

"Heard you have split with Janson.

"You heard right".

"What are you doing now"?

"Making my film".

"Very good".

"Looking for a studio to shoot the film", Arthur said, "Your stodio is empty"?

"My studio was booked for the whole year. But.

"But what"? Arthur said after listening to Robin.

"Watson had booked the studio for a month for the shooting of his film. But now he will not be able to shoot".

"Why"? Arthur said", What happened to Watson".

"Corona", Robin said", He has cancelled the shooting of his film. I haven't given studio to anyone yet. If you want, you can take the studio for a month."

"Thanks", Arthur thanked Robin and said, "You have solved a very big problem".

Arthur's film was long. It was difficult to complete the indoor shooting in a month. All the actors in the film were new. So there was no date problem. Old actors are working in many films simultaneously. So getting date from them, it is difficult. But he did not have this problem.

Arthur started shooting for the film. The actors were new, so retakes had to be done again and again. The entire team worked hard to complete the indoor shooting.

There was a program to go abroad for outdoor shooting. But keeping in mind the budget of the film, the film was shot only in the cities of America. Before the outdoor shooting, the film's poster and a song were released.

Do not touch

me

the meaning of love

No touching or touching

Do not touch

Me

Not necessary

in love

body to body

Do not touch

Me

love not body

comes from the heart

I love you

Your idol

I have kept in my heart

Wherever I live

Love will never be less

Do not touch

Me

As soon as the poster and the song were released, the film started being discussed. The song of the films. The song of the film went on the lips of young men and women.

Arthur completed the shooting of his film before the scheduled time. As soon as the shooting was completed, film went to lab. A month later the final print of the film was ready. The premiere of the film was held in Los Angeles before the film's release. In the premiere, Arthur had invited people from other fields along with media.

"Very good. Excellent".

The people who came to the premiere praised the film. the reviews of the films were published in the newspapers.

And the film was released in America. As soon as it was released, the film created a stir at the box office. People were bored of watching the films of old heroes and heroines. Anichka created a buzz in the first film. The audience coming out of the hall after watching the film would have commented "What a brilliant acting by the heroine". Some says.

The story of the film is also interesting. Every viewer had a different opinion about the film. But all were Unanimous that the film is excellent. Anichka was covered in print, electronic and social media.

"You nailed in the very first film. The film is amazing. The heroine is a wonderful search", One day Johnson's call came to Arthur, "Get the film dubbed in Hindi, Chinese and Japanese as well".

And the film was dubbed in Hindi, Chinese, Japanese and German. languages and released, abroad. The film broke all records at the box office in foreign countries as well. Anichka never thought in her dream that she would capture the hearts of people from the very first film itself. Film magazines would have her photo on the cover page.

"Come on Anichka". One day Arthur had reached Anichka's house. Anichka used to live in a rented flat.

"Where"?

"You come".

Anichka came out with Arthur

"Sit in the car".

"You had an old car. Bought a new car", said Anichka, looking at the car, "When did you buy it"?

"Just brought it from the showroom", Arthur said, "How was the car"?

"Beautiful. Brand new model", Said Anichka sitting in the car.

Arthur had reached a bungalow with Anichka

"Why did you bring me here"?

"To show bungalow".

"Have you bought this too"?

"Yes", Arthur showed Anichka the bungalow and said", Did you like the bunglow".

"Fantastic", said Anichka while admiring the bungalow", appreciation for your choice. Have to give".

"Take it". Arthur said, handling the keys to Anichka.

"Two keys"?

"One of the car and other of the Bungalow".

"Why are you giving me" ?

"This car and bunglow, I bought for you".

"For me"? Ancihka said in surprise, "Why"?

"My very first film is doing tremendous business. The credit for the immeuse success of this film goes to you. People are loving you and your acting.

"You deserve thanks for this", Anichka said", If you didn't make me the heroine in your film. Who would have known me"?

"I am grateful to God for this. He introduced me to you and I liked you at first sight".

"Time is very strong. If the time is bad, bring the person sitting on the top to the ground. If the time is good, bring the person lying on the floor to the floor", Anichka said "Time is what brought me here from Ukraine".

Anichka came to America from England to becaome a heroine. She went to many producers in search of work. Some producers even refused to meet her.

The some producer who wre not ready to take Anichka in their films. When Anichka's first film was a superhit, they were coming to her with offers for their films.

The very first film made Anichka the number one heroine of Hollywood.

"Hey you"? Anichka, seeing Nelson at her house, said. Nelson was a famous hero of Hollywood.

"You did a blast in the first film. What a great acting?.

"Thank you".

Anichka and Nelson were talking when Lucy brought the tea.

Anichka and Nelson were having tea. Then Nelson said", I want to propose you".

Love is a sacred word. A beautiful feeling. Love is the basis of creation. If there is anything beautiful in the world, then it is love. Love of man and woman Every woman falls in love with someone once in her life.

But Ancihka hated the word love. She believed that men are unfaithful. To love a woman into his love trap, he first shows her the vegetable garden.

Don't know how they make promises. A woman surrenders herself under the guise of a man. Men consume women and when they are satisfied, they are thrown out like a fly in milk.

Anichka's mother, Ivana, was a victim of such love. Hearing Nelson's love reqest, Anichka remembers her mother's past which she herself told her.

# VIII

"Hello".

Ivana used to work in a mall. She had a day off on sundays. She used to go for walks. Today she came to the city garden.

Sunday is a holiday. That's why the park is more crowded than other days. Men and Women of all classes and ages come to the park. There are swings etc for children to play in the park. Kept watching the children playing. Then went ahead. In the park lovers were busy in courtship.

Colorful flowers were in gloom in the garden. She came and stood near the roses. She loved red roses. An unknown young man was standing in front of her.

Before Ivana could say anything, the young man said". I am sorry to say, you are very beautiful. More than a rose".

"Thank you", Ivana said with a smile on hearing her praise, "I didn't recognize you"?

"How will you recognize me", The young man said, "We are meeting for the first time".

"That's why"?

"I'm Henry", He said saying his name, "May I know your name"?

"Ivana".

"Very sweet and holy name".

"Where do you live"?

"Philippines".

"You are not from here", Ivana said, "So you have come here to visit"?

"No"

"Then"?

"I have come here to study", said Henry, "I have come here to do Diploma in Mechanical Engineering".

This is How Ivana first met Henry.

"Ivana".

A few days later. Ivana was coming out of a shop. Then she heard a voice. She truned and saw.

"Hey Henry you"?

"Are you in a hurry" ?

"No", Ivana said, "Why"?

"Drink Coffee".

"Let us go".

Ivana walks into the restaurant with Henry.

"Snacks or something else"? Henry sat down and said.

"Only Coffee".

Henry ordered two cups of Coffee.

"How are your studies going"? "Ivana asked. "Good".

The waiter had brought Coffee. They were talking while drinking Coffee.

After that day, Ivana and Henry started meeting Henry's college was closed on Sunday. Ivana also had sundays off. That's why they could meet only on sunday.

One Sunday they were walking in the city garden. Then Ivana said, "What have you seen in Mariopol"?

"Nothing but City Garden".

"There is a lot of to see in the city", Ivana said, "visit the Art Museum".

"When"? Henry asked.

"Next Sunday".

And Ivana took Henry to see the art gallery on sunday.

"This is Arkhip Kuidji". Entering the art gellery, Ivana said pointing to a photo, "This art gallery is named after him".

"Who is this" ? Henry said looking at the photo, "Why is this art gallery named after him" ?

"Was multitalented, rich in unmathed talent. He was born in a very poor family. His parents died when he was six years old". Ivana tells Henry about Kuindzhi, "He struggled through poverty and rose to success".

"All the pictures, paintings etc displayed in the art gallery are of Kuindzhi" ? Henry asked.

"All the paintings, drawings, graphics, letters are safe in this museum".

"Look at this.", Ivana showing one of the paintings to Henry said, "The forest of Russia. They look so natural. Looking at his painting, it seems as if we are actually looking at the forest".

"Look at this. The Sun rising from behind the mountains". Ivana showing Henry second painting said.

"You are very interested in art". Henry said seeing the interest of Ivana's in paintings.

"You are right. I have been a student of art. Drawing has also been my subject. I like Kuindzhi paintings very much. His paintings depict realism and naturalness".

"These paintings look different" ? Henry pointed to one of the paintings.

"Most of the paintings kept in this museum are of Kuindzhi", Ivana said. "Apart from these, the artworks and paintings of Tetiana, Yablonska, Mykhaile, Derehus, Hlusheheuka, Ivan Marchuk, Serhil Shyshka etc. are also displayed here".

Ivana was telling Henry the features of the art gallery as well as the features and characteristics of each of the paintings.

And for several hours Henry spent with Ivana in the art gallery looking at paintings, graphics and other things.

After that day, the process of meeting Henry and Ivana started. Henry was studying in college and Ivana used to work. Both of them had a holiday on sunday, so they could meet only on sunday.

Ivana was fond of travelling. There was no dearth of places to visit in Mariyupol.

There were very old places and heritage sites like museums, gardens, churches, mosques, ports etc. if they did not like going anywhere, they would sit in the restaurant.

Henry's temperament was the opposite of Ivana's. He preferred to sit in a restaurant or park with Ivana than to go for a walk. When Ivana was in front of him, he would gaze at her delicate beauty.

"Why do yoy keep looking at me like this" ? One day Ivana asked Henry.

"Your beauty. Your complexion" Henry spoke after listening Ivana, "God made you in leisure".

"Learn to make some things from you". Ivana smiled after hearing her praise.

"Your smile adds to your beauty". The dimples in Ivana's cheeks added to her beauty when she smiled.

Ivana, when she laughed out loud. Henry would not forget to say to her. "When you laugh, It is as if all the wine have been poured out of the carafe's neck at once".

One day Ivana took Henry for a tour of the port. Big ships and steamers floating in the sea.

Apart from being an industrial area, Mariupol is also centre of higher education. Education here is very cheap.

That's why thousand of students from abroad come here every year to study. Those doing MBBS from Ukraincan can practice in Europe without giving any test.

"Let's go to the zoo next sunday" ? Ivana proposed.

"Yes will go".

On sunday Ivana took Henry to the zoo. Zoo is spread over a very large area. Zoo has wild animals and birds. Sunday is a holiday, so this day is more crowded than other days. Zoo visitors bring fruits etc to feed the animals. Ivana had bought bananas. All the animals and birds are locked in different cages. It is written oniside each cage. Please do not disturb them.

Ivana was fond of traveling. Every sunday she would take Henry somewhere to roam. On the days when they did not go any where, they would sit in a restautant and talk or watch a movie.

One day Henry said to her, "Get me a room to rent".

"Why" ? Ivana said after listening to him. "What will you do with the room" ?

"What do with the room" ? Henry said, "The room is needed for living".

"Who to stay" ?

"Myself".

"You are living. Then why do you need room' ? Ivana said, "Why are you leaving that room" ?

"Why would I leave. That house is close to the college. I don't want to leave it. But I have to leave".

"Why" ?

"The landlord has sold the house".

"So what happened" ? Ivana said, "You have to pay the rent. You pay the rent to the new landlord".

"The new landlord will demolish that house and build a shopping Complex there. Said Henry, "That's why he has asked everyone to vacate the rooms".

"When to vacate the room" ?

"One month later".

"You can live with me. If you don't mind" ? After thinking for a while Ivana said.

"With you" ? Henry spoke after listening to Ivana, "In your house" ?

"Yes".

"Your family won't mind" ?

"There is no one in my house".

"What do you mean" ?

"I am alone".

"You are alone" ?

"Yes", Describing herself Ivana said. "At home and in the world".

"Me to like you", Henry spoke about himself. "I don't mind living with you".

Henry comes to live with Ivana a month later.

Earlier Henry and Ivana used to meet after a week but now they were living together. In the same house. Under one roof.

While living together, they started coming close to each other.

Henry's personality was attractive. Tall, fair complexion and slim body. He was soft spoken and jovial.

Ivana fell in love with Henry. Whether Henry loved her or not. She didn't know. Henry and Ivana were lying in bed one night. Then Henry said, "Say one thing".

"Say".

"You are very beautiful. Angel descended from heaven".

"How many times have you said this".

"Ivana I like you".

"Ok". Ivana shake her head.

"Ivana " I'm love with you".

"Do not make me up".

"Telling the truth", Said Henry, "I like you. I love you".

"Me too". After Henry expressed his love, Ivana spoke.

"You are so sweet". Henry kissed Ivana's delicate lips.

Ivana also replied.

Seeing Ivana's gesture, Henry's courage grew and he started kissing Ivana by filling in his arms.

When two young bodies came near, their breath started heating up. The distance between them disappeared. The two bodies merged into one. Henry first be friended Ivana. Then he became her boy friend while living in a live in relationship with her.

What happened to their physical meeting that night that then every night they started satisfying their physical hunger .

The physical union of man and woman doesn not only result in physical pleasure. The seed of creation is also sown. This is the basis of creation. If there is no new creation, then creation will come to an end. The cycle of life and death goes on continuously on the earth.

One day Ivana woke up in the morning and felt nauseous. Then she realized that her days were numbered. Seeing Ivana nauseous, Henry came to her. "What happened"?

"Same thing that happens with every woman".

"What happens to every woman" ?

"A part of you has made place in my womb".

"What do you mean"? Henry said, looking at Ivana questiningly.

"You idiot", Ivana said holding Henry's nose", I'm going to be the mother of your children".

"Really".

"Yes".

"I'm going to be a father". Henry took Ivana in his arms and started pacing around the room.

"No need to be so happy".

"It is a matter of happiness then why not be happy"?

"We are not married Yet", Ivana said, "If we don't get married, I will either have to become a single mom or have an abortion".

"Neither will you have to have an abortion, not will you be a single mom", Henry said, "We will get married soon".

One day Henry said to Ivana, "Will you come with me to the Philippines after the wedding or I will have to come here".

After thinking for a while, Ivana said. "Do you have any objection to staying here"?

"How do you mind"? Said Henry, "I am as lonely as you are. Whether you go there or I come here. It's the same thing".

"So you come here".

"Then I have to go to the Philippines for a few days".

"Why"?

"When I want to live with you, what will do with the house there", Henry said, "I will sell my house".

"You are right", Ivana said, "when will you come back"?

"As soon as possible".

Henry left for the Philippines, after selling the house and promising to return soon.

# IX

Henry had gone saying to return soon. But slowly three months passed. Henry's phone was also switched off whenever Ivana called.

What with Henry...Somewhere. Something untoward happened to Henry...and the apprehension of untowardness shook. What to do? She didn't know much about Henry. What a strange thing? with whom she had befriended. Was going to be a mother. All she knew about him was that he came from the Philippines.

Philippines is a country in Southeast Asia. Spain has also had authority over this country. This country was named Philippine after the name of king Philip of Spain. Later, Spain leased to America. It got independence from, America in 1946. The population of this country is about. 100 million. Earlier people of Buddism were in majority here. But due to conversion, now ninety percent of the population here is Christian. Coconut and Papaya are grown here in abundance.

After lot of thinking. Ivana decided to go to the Philippine. The decision is taken but where will she go? Philippine is a country of islands, there are more than seven thousand islands.

Where will she find him in so many island. If she finds Henry in one island, her whole life will pass. Then what to do?

She could not understand how to go to the Philippines to find, Henry. After much thought. Ivana thought of Henry's collage.

Henry used to study in the collage. While taking admission in the college, he must have written the address in the admission form. And she got the formula to find Henry.

And Ivana went to the college and met the principal and told him her problem.

"You will get information from the office". On the advice of the principal, Ivana met the college clerk. After listening to her the clerk had taken out the old admission forms.

"There are two Henry. Which Henry's address do you want" ? The clerk showed both the forms to Ivana and said.

"Its". Photograph were affixed on the admission form. After seeing both the photograph, Ivana said keeping her hand on one photo.

"Quezon city". The clerk wrote down the address and gave it to Ivana.

To go abroad, along with passport, visa of that country is also required. She had to run for a month to get passport and visa. And one day she get on a plane to the Philippines. She reached Quazon city. It is the most populous city in the Philippines.

"Uncle know it" ?

After asking from place to place, Ivana reached the address which she had got from the college.

The door of the house was closed. She rang the door bell.

"Who are you ? Who do you want to meet" ? The man who opened the door asked her.

"I'm Ivana . . . " said Ivana describing herself. "Henry lives here" ?

"Lived".

"Doesn't live now"? Ivana said after listening to that man.

"Yes".

"But I was given the address of this place". Showing the paper to the man Ivana said, "Isn't this house Henry's"?

"The house used to be Henry's. But not now", said the man, "Henry sold this house to me".

"Do you know where Henry lives now".

"Manila'.

"Did you know the address of manila".

"Yes". The man told Ivana. Henry's Manila address.

Henry had come asking Ivana to sell the house. He had sold the house as well. But after the selling the house, instead of going to Ukraine, he went to Manila. Why ?

She had heard that man are also unfaithful. First they trap a woman in the trap of love. A woman has natural weakness she trusts a man's words very quickly. And in this trust she is cheated. This is the reason that the woman is also forced to be a single mom.

Some where she also did not become a victim of infidelity. Some where Henry also did not play with her by trapping her in the trap of love. He did not cheat her. Many such questions were emerging in her mind while coming to Manila from Quezon city.

And she reached Henry's house.

"This is henry's house" ? When the bell rang, a young woman opened the door. Ivana asked her.

"Yes".

"Will call them" ?

"Henry is not at home", that young woman said, "Went to work".

"Where does Henry work" ?

"In the motor company". The young woman told Ivana about Henry's motor company.

"Who are you" ? Ivana asked the young woman.

"I am Alisha", Alisha said introducing herself. "I am Henry's wife".

Knowing about Alisha the ground slipped from under Ivana's feet. There was a fear and a doubt in her mind while coming to Philippines. The way she was thinking before coming here the same happened to her. After playing with her feelings, her body and her love. Henry had come to his country by making excuses from her.

After discovering Henry infidelity, Ivana thought. Now what will she do by going to Henry. He is now married, then a thought came to her mind. It is necessary to remove the mask of decency from Henry's face. She came to the Philippines only for Henry. Then why did she return without meeting him. And she went to meet Henry.

Henry did not return to Ukraine, nor did his phone call. Then Ivana was terrified. Fears of untoward thing started haunting her. That's why she came to the Philippines.

She found out when she came here. Her fears, her apprehension were unfounded. Nothing had happened to Henry. He had betrayed Ivana. Had cheated in love. Played with her identity by creating a drama of love. Had consumed her.

Men are unfaithful. First they creat a drama of love and trap the woman. Then when the woman becomes pregnant, they leave her. Such men are there in every country. There was no dearth of such men in her country. But she did not even dreem that she would get such a man.

Why blame Henry. She herself was to blame. She made a mistake in recognizing Henry. Even after being in a live in relationship, she could not recognize him. Before surrendering, she did not think thatHenry could also commit infidelity.

Thinking in her mind Ivana want to Henry.

"You" ? Henry was stunned to see Ivana.

"It's a surprise to see me", said Ivana, looking at Henry, "You would not expect me to be here".

Seeing Ivana Henry did not know what to say to her.

"You had come after promising me to come back. Far from returning, you switched off your mobile". Seeing Henry silent, Ivana spoke again.

"My phone . . ."

"There is no need to lie or make any excuses", Ivana interrupted Henry's speech and said, "I was worried about you, when you did not return. May something untoward happened to you. And this worry took me to you".

Henry was silent.

"If you did not want to marry me, then why do you promise to marry me ? Why did you playwith my pride"? Ivana said angrily, "played with my body and married another woman"?

"Sit Ivana. I will tell you every thing".

"Now what is left to tell", Ivana was angry. "If you were in my country, I would tell you what is the consequence of messing with woman".

Henry tried hard to stop Ivana but she did not stop.

While going to Philippines, Ivana had fear, apprehension and eagerness and curiosity to go to her lover's country.

The fear and apprehension in Ivana's mind about Henry proved to be baseless. She got to go there and see her lover's infidelity.

Ivana had different questions on her way to the Philippines and different ones on her return.

When Henry was living with her, she was so happy to be pregnant. Every woman is happy. A woman is complete only after becoming a mother. When she became pregnant. She began to dream of the future.

Henry's infidelity had forced Ivana to think. The child who was growing in her womb earlier as a sign of love, now she was seeing the fruit of sin.

After thinking for several days, Ivana decided that she would not give birth to a child. She would not allow the child of an unfaithful man to come in to this world.

Due to her decision a conflict broke out between her and her soul.

She wanted to drop the child but her spirit was preventing her from doing so.

The struggle between Ivana and her soul goes on.

Ivana's conscience tried hard to persuade her but Ivana did not listen to her conscience and went to Dr. Lisa.

"Doctor, I want to have abortion".

"Why" ?

When asked by Dr. Lisa, she told the reason for the abortion.

"What is the child's fault in this" ? said Dr. Lisa explaining to Ivana, "Think again" .

"I have come after much thought".

"As you wish".

Doctor Lisa got some test and ultrasound done for Ivana. After seeing of the report of test and ultrasound, Doctor Lisa said, "You drop the idea of abortion".

"Why" ?

"It's risky. It could even kill you".

"No problem", said Ivana after listening to Dr. Lisa."I do not care about my life".

"Sorry", Doctor Lisa said, "I can't put your life in danger".

Dr. Lisa flatly refuses abort Ivana. After Dr. Lisa's refusal. Ivana met many doctors but no doctor was ready to take the risk.

Ivana did not want to give birth to her unfaithful lover Henry's child. she had to give birth to the child even though she did not want to and she became a single mom. Mother of a daughter.

Motherhood is the desire of every woman. Still she first wanted to get rid of the womb. But after becoming a mother, mother's love awakened in her heart.

Her daughter was more beautiful than her. So she named the daughter Anichka.

Ivana loved her daughter very much. seeing her daughter, she also remembered her unfaithful lover.

"What are you thinking"?

Hearing Nelson voice, she was broughtback from the past to the present.

"Sorry Nelson".

Anichka rejected Nelson's marriage proposal.

# X

Smith was the superstar of hollywood. Heroines were eager to work with him. Anichka was working in a film with the same Smith.

The story of the film was based on married life. In this film, Anichka became Smith's wife.

The film was based on the love afair of husband and wife. The outdoor shooting of the film was done in France and Italy apart from America. The film also had bedroom, bathroom and rainy scenes. There were also romantic and sexy scene. Smith began to feel intimate while shooting with Anichka. Smith was an attractive young man of tall stature, slim body. His every film was a hit. There was no dearth of girls who wanted him. Don't know how many girls had proposed marriage to him after requesting him for love. But he didn't accept anyone offer. The Smith who was wanted by millions of girls. The Smith who did not give lift to any girl. The same Smith fell in love with Anichka. One day while shooting a scene, Smith said to Anichka, "I have fallen in love with you".

"Really"?

"Yes Anichka. I am in love with you".

"There is nothing wrong with loving".

"I want to make you mine".

"Means marriage".

"Yes".

"Sorry".

Don't know how many girls marriage proposals had been rejected by Smith. The same Smith's proposal was turned down by Anichka.

Many more had proposed to her before Smith.

Whenever a man proposes to Anichka, she remembers her mother's past and she rejects his proposal.

"You act amazing".

Arthur threw a party on the grand success of his first film. Apart from the film world and media, people from other fields were also invited in this party.

"Your acting is wonderful. Your acting is less to be praised". A man of attractive personality came to her and said.

"Thanks", Anichka thanked the man and said", We are probably meeting for the first time. May I know your introduction"?

"This is Johnson", Before Johnson could say something, Arthur came near and said, "He is the distributor and financier. He had financed our film. He also suggested dubbing the film in Hindi, Chinese etc".

"Pleased to meet you". Anichka said.

"You live here"?

"New Youk", Johnson spoke", I have to go to New Jersey. Arthur's request had to come".

Johnson and Anichka were talking. Food, drink, dance and music was also going on.

"I'm sorry. I don't feel like leaving you But what should I do. It's time for my flight", After sometime, Johnson said, "Good bye to Anichka", I'll see you again soon".

And Johnson was gone. Anichka was a heroine. She used to meet many people every day. But no one impressed her. But Johnson had cast a spell on her in the very first meeting. One night Anichka's phone rang.

"Hello". Anichka said holding the mobile to her ear.

"Johnson", A voice came from the other end, "Recognized".

"How can I forget my well wisher", Anichka said happily. "How are You"?

"Fine", said Johnson, "the day after tomorrow is the time"?

"Why"?

"I'm coming to Los Angeles the day after tomorrow", Johnson said, "I'd like to see you if you have time".

"Time can be taken".

Anichka had cancelled all the shoots for that day.

Anichka used to wake up early on that day when she had to go for the shoot. But today she woke up comfortably. She had bought a new dress to wear today.

Johnson flight was at one O' clock in the afternoon. She decided to go to the airport to receive Johnson.

She was very curiouse about Johnson. And she reached the airport at twelve O' clock. Anichka wanted to surprise Johnson. That's why she didn't tell Johnson about coming to the airport.

Anichka had come to the airport an hour eralier. She knew that if she got out of the car, her fans would mob her. So she remained seated in the car. The flight form New York arrived at its scheduled time. Like as the passengers started getting off the plane. Anichka walked into the lounge. As soon as she caught sight of Johnson, she shouted, "Johnson".

"Anichka", Johnson. happy to see Anichka, said "What a surprise"? I didn't even think that you would came to recieve me".

"If I had told you about my arrival then where would the surprise be".

"You are right".

Anichka took Johnson to the Hotel Hyatt for lunch. She had made special dishes for Johnson. While eating Johnson said, "Your taste in food is wonderful".

"Liked the food"?

"Very tasty and delicious".

Anichka and Johnson were talking while eating. Johnson had left and impression on Anichka's heart from the very first meeting. That impression was getting deeper in the second meeting.

"Are you not shooting any of your films in New York" ?

"One day outdoor shooting to happen next month".

"Let me know when you are coming", said Johnson, "I shall be glad to welcome you".

And did not realize. When the time passed. Johnson had to return at night itself. Anichka had gone to the airport to see him off.

After that day, Anichka started talking to Johnson. Whenever Anichka got time, she did not forget to call him. Sometimes she could not call, then Johnson's phone would come.

One day Anichka called Johnson, "Tomorrow I'm coming to New York for a shoot".

"I'll come to receive you", Johnson said, "What's the program"?

The whole team is coming. Some scenes are to be shot in New York. At night the whole team will go to London for outdoor shooting, "Anichka said" you come. See the shooting also and we will talk".

"Ok".

The film was to be shoot at the "Statue of Liberty", and "Central Park", Johnson, had cancelled all his program for the day to watch the film shoot and meet Anichka.

The entire team of the film had reached New York in the morning. Johnson had reached the airport. But could talk to Anichka for a few minutes. The film began shooting shortly after the team arrived in New York.

Johnson was present throughout the shooting. Anichka was free in the evening. Then Johnson said, "Let's go to dinner".

Johnson took Anichka to the Hampton Hotel. Johnson had already booked a table for dinner. "I love the dinner in this hotel".

"Why"? Anichka said sitting down.

"You'll know for yourself when you eat"?

The waiter started bringing plates of food on the table.

"Have it". Johnson urged Anichka to eat. They started eating. They were talking while eating.

"Liked food"? Johnson asked after eating.

"The food is really awesome".

While eating and taking, they did not realize when the time passed. Anichka looked at her wrist watch and said, "It's time for the flight".

Anichka had already told the director that she would go straight to the airport without coming to the hotel.

"Now let's go" ? Anichka said getting up.

"Let's us go" ?

Anichka got into the car with Johnson. The car started running on the streets of New york. The night was worth seeing in the colourful lights of New York city. And the car reached the airport.

"Bye". Anichka got down from the car and went away waving.

After that day, Anichka and Johnson started meeting frequently. Anichka could not go to New York due to her busy schedule. But Johnson started coming to Los Angeles after two to four days to meet her.

One day Johnson and Anichka were sitting in the hotel, then Johnson expressed his love and said, "I want to propose you".

"Means marriage".

"Yes", said Johnson, "I want to marry you".

"What is the use. We will not be able to live together even after marriage".

"Why" ?

"I am in Los Angeles and you are in New York", Anichka said, "I don't want to leave acting now. I have achieved this position with hard work.

"I'm not asking you to quit acting". Johnson said, "You come to New York when you're not shooting. I'll come to you when I'm free".

Earlier, if someone proposed to Anichka, she would remember her mother past. And she would immediately reject the marriage proposal.

But she was impressed by Johnson for two reasons. First he had a charming personality and was soft spoken and tactful. Second Johnson despite not being introduced to Anichka played an important role in making her popular outside Anichka by suggesting her first film to be dubbed in Hindi, Chinese etc. language.

That's why Anichka accepted Johnson's Marriage proposal.

# XI

Anichka and Johnson's wedding ceremony was held at St. Vieente's Church. Anichka had invited only a few people to attend the wedding ceremony.

Anichka had stitched a white dress for the wedding. She look like an angel descended from heaven in this dress. Johnson ware a red suit. He looked like a prince in this suit.

Pastor Jaime had completed the marriage rituals of Anichka and Johnson in the church.

Anichka had organized a dinner party at hotel Aizalono. In this party, degnitaries from other fields were also invited along with big personlities of the film world.

People started coming to the hotel as soon as the night fall. Anichka came to the party in a red dress and Johnson in a blue suit. As soon as both of them entered hand to hand, hotel burst in to applause resounded.

"This is Smith . . ."

Anichka started introducing Johnson to the guests. The invited guests were congratulating them on the wedding as well as giving them gifts.

Media persons were also present in the party.

Johnson had already asked Anichka. "Where to go far the honeymoon"?

"As you like".

"Not me", Johnson said, "You tell".

"I will tell", Anichka said after thinking for a while Switzerland.

"O K".

Johnson had booked tickets and hotel for Switzerland online. They had a 2 A.M flight out of Los Angeles.

The party went on until 12 A. M. At the end of the party Anichka spoke to her manager Heath, "We have to catch a flight. We are leaving. You take all the gifts to the bungalow",

"OK madam".

Anichka and Johnson came to the airport with their luggage from the bungalow. After boarding the plane, Anichka had asked Johnson, "In which city of Switzerland has the hotel been booked" ?

"Zurich".

"Have you been to Switzerland before".

"No", Johnson said turning his head and looking to Anichka. "And you" ?

"So far none of my films have been shot in Switzerland "Anichka said, "I am also going for the first time".

Anichka started reading about Switzerland in Google.

Switzerland is a country situated in the hills of the Alps in the middle of Europe. This country is famous in the world for its natural beauty. It is because of the natural beauty that it is called, "Heaven of the Earth".

Everyone dreams of coming to Switzerland. Everyone want to see the heaven of earth with their own eyes. Millions of tourists come here every year.

Switzerland is the first choice of newly weds for honeymoon.

This country has beautiful snow capped mountains, natural lakes, gleciers, pastures and valleys, which are full of colorful flowers and trees with difference types of leaves.

This country is very suitable place for nature, lovers and trekking, skating.

Johnson and Anichka had reached Zurich. This city is the capital of Switzerland as well as a commercial and cultural centre.

Anichka said as soon as she reached the hotel, "I am very tired. Today I will not go any where" ?

"As you like".

And that day Anichka did not leave the hotel room at all. She had gone to sleep after having breakfast.

Johnson also rested in the room. In the evening he had gone out of the hotel for some time.

"Have booked hotel for four days". Anichka wake up for dinner then Johnson said, "Today's day passed in the hotel itself".

"Will go tomorrow", Anichka said, While eating food, "When to go tomorrow"?

"The car will come at nine".

"O K".

In the morning, Anichka and Johnson got ready after having breakfast. At nine o'clock the car was parked in the hotel compound. The guide was also with him.

"Where are you taking today" ? While sitting in the car Anichka asked the guide.

"Mater Horn Peak".

And the guide took them to the Mater Horn Peak.

"It is a mountain of the Alps mountain Range", the guide spoke, "about the mountain", Its peak is the highest in Europe.

"Really"? After listening to the guide, Anichka said, "What is the height of the peak"?

"Four thousand four hundred and eighteen meters".

"It is more than a thirteen thousand feet high". Johnson said.

"The summit of this mountain is the most difficult climb. More than five hundred climbers have lost their lives in an attempt to reach the summit. But the spirit of the climbers has not diminished". The guide was telling them.

"Many tourists come here". Pointing to the tourists Anichka said.

"Tourists used to come here earlier also. But after the construction of the railway line in this area, the number of tourists has increased a lot".

"The snow covered hills are looking so beautiful". Anichka said.

"Films are also being shot. here". The guide was telling every small and big thing to Anichka and Johnson.

"And this is the thiohul pass".

"What is this use"?

"After the Roman Empire, trade was carried out through this pass". And they didn't even know when it was evening while roaming there.

It was night time by the time they came back to the hotel. And at night Johnson and Anichka...

"Where are you taking today"? The next day while sitting in the car Johnson asked the guide.

"Utlivarg mountain".

"Where is it"? Anichka had spoken.

"It is at a height. It will take us an hour to reach there".

The car was galloping on the road. Anichka was looking outside. It was a beautiful sight. Beautiful trees with colorful flowers and leaves.

"This is a famous entertainment place here", The guide got down from the car and pointed towards the tourists and said", There is such a crowd here throughtout the year. Tourists come from all over the country and abroad".

"The atmosphere here is quite cool".

"There is also an ideal trekking spot for people who are fond of wlking", The guide told about there, "From here you can also see a panoramic view of the whole city and lake".

Toursists were walking around looking at the view of the city and the lake. Anichka said while walking with her husband. "Take selfies".

Johnson came and stood beside Anichka "come a little closer".

Anichka took selfie with her husband and also alone.

"Now let me show you, The Rhine Falls", The guide took them to the Rhine Falls.

"Here the water is falling very fast". Looking at the water Anichka said.

"This is the most powerful waterfall in Europe. Here the water falls at the fastest speed. It is believed that this waterfall is more than seventeen thousand years old". The guide was telling them about the waterfall.

The guide also showed them the Lugano Lake. The beauty of this lake is made on sight. This lake is counted among the most beautiful places in Switzerland. Switzerland is on one side of this lake and Italy on the other. Millions of tourists come here every year.

The guide also took them to Interlaken village, Lucney and Lake Geneva. Lake Geneva is near the border of France and Switzerland. It is the largest lake here. The snow capped mountains along its banks offer a very beautiful view.

Johnson and Anichka return to Los Angeles after completing a week long honeymoon tour. Johnson stayed with Anichka for a day and then moved to New York.

One day Johnson called and said to Anichka, "You have given a wedding party to your friends. My friends are also asking for a party".

"So give party".

"Which day are you free from shooting". I hold a party on the same day.

"Don't worry about my shooting. Keep the day you want. I will adjust". Anichka had given her approval for the party.

Johnson had organized a dinner party at Hotel Hyatt. Apart from his friends, he had invited big businessmen, politicians and other dignitaries of the society to the party.

Anichka had become a very big star. People used to see her on the screen of the film. But in the party they would get a chance to see her face to face. That's why no one wanted to miss the party.

"Meet them".

Johnson started introducing Anichka to the people who came to the party.There was arrangement for drinks and dance along with dinner in the party. The hotel hall was packed. People were standing in small groups and talking. Women were also standing in groups.

"How did such a big star get trapped by this lumpen". A woman's whisper was lying in Anichka's ears.

"Debauched. Completely debauched, that's why Maria left". Another woman's whisper was heard.

"No woman can tolerate her husband flying around with other women". Anichka's ears perked up at the whispering of the women.

Anichka was thinking of Johnson as a gentleman, a good man, But the cheerfulness of the women was telling different story.

Are the words of women true? Should she believe what she has heard? May be the women who do bad things about Johnson are jealous of him. Tha'ts why they are accusing Johnson.

Many such questions arose in her mind after listening to those women.

She decided to find out the truth herself rather than believe what she heard.

When Anichka woke up in the morning, Morrison brought a tray of tea.

"Good morning".

"Morning", Anichka replying to the greeting, "Where is Johnson"?

"Sir has gone somewhere for work".

"How long have you been here"?

"Since ten years"

"Who was Maria"? Anichka asked a direct question without any prepositions.

"Sir's first wife".

Anichka found out as much as she knew about Maria form Morrison. Maria lived in Cape Town. Anichka went to Cape town one day to meet Maria "What a wonder? I am not dreaming"? Maria was happy to see Anichka.

"This is not a dream".

"Reality is like a dream come true", said Maria, "The one whom people yearn to get a glimpse of is in front of me today".

"Sometimes the well has to go to the thirsty".

"So you have come to me for some purpose", Maria said after listening to Anichka, "What can I be of use to you"?

"Johnson"...

"Don't talk to me about that scoundrel . . . Maria got angry on hearing Johnson's name.

"Maria I've come to you from Los Angeles to talk to you about that same Johnson. He's been your husband, so who knows better about him than you, "Anichka said", Now he is my "Husband".

"You are such a big star, don't know how you got trapped in his love".

"Maria, I made a big mistake. I don't know what he did that clouded my conscience. He didn't tell me that he was a divorce. I came to know about his antics from other women at the party, "Anichka said", Why did you divorce him"?

"Specializes in entrapping women in his trap. He is dissolute. He has relations with so many women, Can't tolerate her husband flying around with other women, "Maria said in a harsh voice" What is the use of living with such a man. Who does not respect the feelings of his wife".

Anichka regrets her decision when she learns Johnson's reality from Maria. Her mother was deceived by Henry on the pretext of love. Due to the infidelity with the mother if was brought home in her mind that all men are unfaithful. That is why she did not want to get married and had rejected all the men's proposals before Johnson. But don't know what spell Johnson had put on her that she could not reject his proposal.

Anichka loved Johnson but hated him after his exploits came to light.

Anichka started quarreling with her husband over illegal relations with other women.

But Johnson did not improve. Earlier Anichka used to call Johnson daily but now she has stopped calling.

One day Anichka reached New York without informing her husband "Who is she"? Seeing Johnson in the bedroom with another woman, Anichka asked ?

"Naney".

"What is she doing in your bedroom"?

"She is living in live in relationship with me".

"Married and living with another woman".

"What should I do if you don't live with me? Need a bed partner".

"I told you before marriage, I will not be able to stay together".

"Don't stay, but let it be". Anichka did not want Nancy to stay with Johnson, while Johnson did not to expel her. This led to a quarrel between them. When Johnson could not get enough, he said, I am a man".

"So"? Anichka said staring at him.

"I do whatever I want? Who are you to stop me"?

"If you are a man then I am also a woman".

"What will you do if you are a woman"?

"I will answer you in your own language".

And Anichka went back angrily.

# XII

As soon as the first films became a hit. Anichka had a line of films. Every producer wanted to take her in his film.

She was working in many films simultaneously. So she was very busy. Films had indoor as well as outdoor shooting. Outdoor shooting of a films was to be done in kashmir and Mumbai. The team of the film came to India for the shooting. Three days of shooting was to be done Srinagar, Baramulla and Gulbarga in Kashmir.

Seeing the natural scenery of Kashmir like Switzerland, lakes, water falls and picturesque valleys laden with flowers. Anichka really felt that Kashmir is heaven on earth. The shikara floating on Dal lake fascinated her.

The team had come to Mumbai after shooting for three days in Kashmir.

Mumbai is Indian's metropolies, the country's financial capital. City of dreams. Bollywood, the centre of Hindi films. The set was ready for shooting at the Gateway of India. Shooting of Boolywood films used to happen daily in Mumbai. But shooting of Hollywood films used to happen only occasionally.

Hollywood movies have their own craze. Now Hollywood movies are being dubbed in Hindi as well. Even when there was no dub, there was no dearth of fans of Hollywood movies.

People came to know about the shooting of a Hollywood films in Mumbai from the newspapers. That's why a large number of people came to watch the shooting.

When Anichka came on the set, her eyes went to the crowd of people who had come to watch the shooting. Not many people come to America. Her eyes were on a youngman. That youngman broke the security cardon of the police and made a place in the crowd and come forward. He started moving towards the set, then a policeman's eyes fell on him. He hold his hand and stipped him saying, "Where are you going" ?

"I want to meet heroine" ?

"You can't go on" ?

"I will go" ?

The policeman didn't want to let him go even though he was insisting on meeting the heroine.Seeing his insistence, the policeman said, "You did't love your life".

"My soul lives in her. I want to meet her. I want to talk to her".

"Now I will exercise the ghost of your lover". The policeman took him away with a stick.

"The set is ready"? Then the voice of director was heard.

"Yes".

"Camera ready"?

Everyone got ready for the shoot as soon as they heard the director's voice.

"Action".

And the shooting started. After a long time when the shooting was over, Anichka looked at the crowd, but the young man was not visible to her. She had come to the hotel with her team.

Even now she was thinking only about that young man. She was very impressed with that young man. He was her true admirer. He was even ready to get beaten up by the police to meet her.

She wanted to meet that young man. But how? She had only caught a glimpse of him in the crowd. After thinking for a while, she called the cameraman Robert, "Did you turn the camera towards the people who came to watch the shooting"?

"That was not a part of the scene", After listening to Anichka, Robert said, "Why are you asking"?

"I want to meet a young man who came to see the shooting". Anichka told Robert the reason for asking.

"I didn't turn the camera towards the people who came to see the shooting", Robert said, "May be George took photos of the crowd"?

"Who is George"?

"American press reporter posted in Mumbai".

"You can call him"?

"Why not"?

George came running as soon as he heard that Anichka had called. After listening to Anichka George said, "Nobody takes photos of the people who came to see the shooting. Still, I talk to the journalists who came there".

And George was gone.

The shooting in Mumbai was only for one day. But the team stayed of two more days to visit. Mumbai and meet Bollywood stars.

About fifty Indian and foreign journalists had come to cover the shooting of the Hollywood film, George was living in Mumbai, so he knew everyone. George spoke to everyone on the phone. But no one took photographs of the people who came to see the shooting.

Next day Anichka called George, "Found out something"?

"Not yet". George said, "I am busy with your work".

After much effort, George came to know about Laxman. Laxman was neither a press reporter not a freelancer. He was a fan of Hollywood films.

He had gone to see the shooting and also clicked photographs there. George came to know about him from a journalist of Mumbai.

George reached Laxman's house. Knowing the introduction of George, Laxman said, "What can I do for you"?

George told Laxman the reason for his arrival. After listening to George, Laxman brought all the photos and gave them to George.

George went to Anichka with those photos.

"Thank you. You have helped me a lot", Anichka said thanking George, "I will not forget it". After George left, Anichka started looking at those photos again. She found the young man in a photo. After finding that young man in the photo, Anichka called the hotel manager.

"You called me"?

"Yes", Anichka said, "I need your help".

"Tell me", Hotel manager. Narang had said.

"You are looking at this young man"? Anichka had shown the photo to Narang.

"Yes". Looking at the photo, Narang said.

"I want to meet this young man".

"So meet him. What's the problem with that"?

"I don't know this young man. I saw him in the crowd of people who came to watch the shooting", Anichka said to Narang, "I want to know about this young man".

"Madam, Mumbai is a metropolitan city. Its population is more than two crores. Finding a person in Mumbai without name and address is as impossible as finding a needle in a sea".

"Anyhow I want to meet this young man. Please help me". Anichka begged Narang. Narang got into thinking after listening to Anichka. After thinking for a while he suddenly said", We can find him with a trick".

"What trick"?

"Nowadays it is the era of social Media. You put this young man's photo on social media. Somebody must know him".

"Narang, you are absolutely right. After listening to Narang, Anichka said", this thing did not even come to my mind".

Anichka followed. Narang's suggestion and within a few hours Anichka had come to know about the young man.

The name of that youngman was Anuj and he used to work in a company at Churchgate.

Anichka wished she could have called the youngman to meet her. But she did not to do so. She herself went to Anuj.

"Ma'am we have come".

She was brought back from the past to the present when she heard the driver voice.

"And Anichka got down from the car and went to Anuj's house.

# XIII

"You are Anichka"? Neerja was surprise to see Anichka in her house.

Even after listening to Neerja, when Anichka did not say anything, then she said agian, "You are a famous heroine of Hollywood"?

"You recognized me"?

"Why won't you recognize. My husband is a big fan of yours. He likes your movie live in relation with celebratory".

"Yor are telling the truth"?

"See with your own eyes". Neerja took Anichka's hand and took her to her bedrooms.

Anuj's bedroom had pictures of her all around. Anichka suddenly could not believe that there is a love for her even across the seven seas. He is crazy about her. He is a fan of her. Looking at the bedroom with incredulous eyes, she said, "You are right. Your husband is a big fan of mine".

"Why has my husband kept your pictures in the bedroom"? Neerja looked at Anichka questioningly.

"Why"? Anichka answered Neerja's question with a question.

"In our country, it is believed that the son continues the lineage. That's why every couple wants only a son to be born to them", Neerja said, "But my husband does not want that".

"So what does Anuj want"?

"He wants a daughter to be born from my womb".

"This thinking is good", Anichka said. "Creation in done only by women. If there is no woman, then how will a son be born"?

"Do you know what kind of daughter my husband wants"? Neerja had said.

"What kind of daughter does he want"? Anichka had asked Neerja.

"Like you".

"Like me", Anichka said with astonishment. "Anuj wants a daughter, but like me".

"Yes. Just like you", Neerja said, "That's why my husband has kept your photos in the bedroom"?

"Wow". Anichka was pleasantly surprised and happy to hear Neerja's words.

"I started talking about myself", Neerja said, "In my talk, I forgot to ask why you have come to me"?

"I have come to you for a work".

"To me for work" Neither you know me, nor I know you. Then how did you come to me and how can I be of use to you"?

"I have met Anuj before coming to you".

"You went to my husband".

"I went to your husband before coming to you".

"Then"?

"Your husband is not ready for what I say".

"What is the work that my husband could not do and you had to come to me"?

"You can do that".

"Really. I can", Neerja said, "What is the work that I can do"?

"I want to live in relationship with your husband".

"What"? Neerja listening to Anichka, said with astonishment, "What did you say. Say it once again".

"I want to be in a live in relationship with your husband". Anichka reiterated her point again.

"Oh Now I get it".

"What did you understand"?

"You want to take my husband away from me".

"Neerja, you are understanding wrong. I do not want to snatch your husband from you", Anichka said, "I want to be in live in relation with you husband".

"The thing is the same. The trend of live in relationship has started in our country too. Boys and girls are not getting married and are living in live-in-relaionship. Men and women live together like husband and wife without being bound by marriage. Once my husband leaves me then he is not going to come back to me".

"As you are thinking, it will not happen".

"Why won't it happen? You are such a big star. If he starts living with you, then why would he leave you? He will go from the hut to the palace, then leaving the life of luxury, why will he come back to me to live a life of poverty"?

"Neerja I want to be in live in relationship with your husband. Only for six months. If you don't believe me then we can make a legel contract".

"But why do you want to live with my husband only. You are such a big star, anyone will be ready to line with you".

"Neerja you are absolutely right. Anyone will be ready to be with me. But I have liked Anuj only", Anichka said, "After coming to your house, my intention to stay with your husband has became more firm".

Knowing Anichka's intention, Neerja said, "I am a house wife. If you take my husband with you, how I will survive" ?

"Don't worry. I'll give you fifty thousand dollars a month" ?

Fifty thousand dollars. Means three lakh dollars in six month. After listening to Anichka, Neerja started calculating in her mind. If three lacs dollars are converted into rupees than it will be more then two crore rupees. And she remembered her past.

Neerja was born in a lower middle class family in Vadodara. Her father worked in a company. She was the eldest of four sisters. It is considered the responsibility of the parents to marry a daughter here. Her father had given her higher education thinking that she would get a good groom it she was highly educated.

Every girl starts dreaming of her future as soon as she steps on the threshold of youth. Today's every educated girl has a dream, she gets a doctor, engineer, officers or businessman as a life partner. Neerja also had a similar dream of her future.

Dreams are the illusion of closed eyes which never come true. neerja was beautiful as well as highly educated. Her father also wanted her to get a doctor, engineer or officer boy as son-in-law.

No matter how beautiful, educated and qulafied a girl is here ? It is not possible for her to marry a good and capable boy without dowry. The higher the status and good job of the boy, the higher the demand for dowry. Now a day doctor, engineers or to make a government officer son-in-law, at least sixty-seventy lakh rupees are needed. Neerja's father's salary used to cover the household expenses, then from where did he get so much money to marry his daughter to a high ranking boy ?

Even after making a lot of efforts, the father could not find such a son-in-law as he wanted. It did not mean that the daughter would remain a virgin at home. Then he started looking for a son-in-law of her level.

Thirty to fourty lakh rupees were also required for the daughter's marriage to a middle class government servent boy. At last their search stopped on Anuj.

Anuj had no one in this world. Nither ancestral property nor his own house. He worked in a company in mumbai and lived in a rented house. There was no demand for dowry.

Neerja's dream was broken when she saw in her bachelorhood. Neerja who was dreaming of a bungalow. Come to her husband's small rented house after marriage. Mumbai Mayanagari city of dreams.

Where on one side there are buildings touching the sky. On the other side are chalas and slum huts. Where on one side there are rich people running on the roads in fast cars. On the other side there are common people travelling by hanging in local trains. On one side there is happiness and on the other side there is despair. On one side there is richness and on the other side there is poverty.

Marriage is considered a sacred bond in our country. A bond in which a man and a woman become husband and wife for life. Neerja was dreaming of living a life of luxury after marriage. But she had to settle for a boy doing a minor job in the company. She had to live with her husband in a rented house for the rest of her life. Due to her husband's low income, she could not dream of her own house in the city of Mumbai.

But Anichka's proposal had revived. Neerja's dream of living a life of luxury and having her own house before marriage. She started thinking in her mind. What to do ? Accept Anichka's proposal or not ?

"Where are you lost Neerja" ? Hearing Anichka's voice, she came back from the past to the present and asked, "Anuj will come back" ?

"Neerja, I have already told you. I want to take your husband with me only for six months".

"You are telling the truth" ?

"Don't be afraid. I am also married like you. Your husband is faithful to you but not my husband. My husband is promiscuous. He has illicit relations with so many women".

"Now he has also brought a woman with whom he is living in live-in-relationship. I do not want to live with such a man even for a moment". Explaining the reason for taking Anuj along. She said, "But before breaking up with my husband. I want to answer him in his on language".

Neerja know that her husband loves her deeply. He is completely devoted to her. He will never be ready to live with another woman.

But Anichka's three lakh dollar were floating in front of Neerja's eyes. The value of three lakh dollar in Anichka was only three lakhs. But when Neerja will get three lakh dollars, then in Indian rupees their value will be more than two crore rupees.

Two crores do not matter to those who have crores to spare. But Neerja did not even have a thousand rupees in her bank account. Two crores was a huge amount for her. Her husband could not add so much money from his job even in his whole life.

With the money, she got from Anichka, she could fulfil her dream of bachelorhood. With these money, she could buy a house and other luxury items. she could start some work of her own. Neerja said after thinking for a while, "I accept your proposal" ?

"You agree but will Anuj agree" ?

"He has refused you, so it is not easy to convince him", Neerja said, "But you leave that to me. It is my responsibility to convince my husband".

"If you have faith, you can convince your husband, then take this". Anichka said giving fifty thousand dollars to Neerja". Every month you will continue to get fifty thousand dollars.

Anichka had gone. The film team had returned to America. But Anichka stayed back in Mumbai.

When Anuj returned home in the evening, seeing the dollars in his wife's hand, he said, "From where did you get so much foreign currency" ?

"Anichka'.

"She had come here" ? Anuj said after listening to his wife.

"Yes".

"Why did she came here" ?

"She went to you too". Neerja answered her husband's question with a question. "Why did she go to you" ?

"She wants to live in relationship with me".

"And you refused", Neerja said after listening to her husband. "That's why she came to me".

"What did you say" ?

Neerja did not say anything through her mouth. Holding the dollar in her hand, she handed over to her husband.

"Means you have accepted Anichka's proposal' Understanding wife's gesture. Anuj said "

Yes. Anichka is a Hollywood superstar. Anyman would be ready to have a live in relationship with her. But she has liked you, she wants to be with you only because you are her true fan. Proof of which she's seen during the shooting and in your bedroom. You should be happy. You are getting a chance to be with the person whom people crave to talk to, "Neerja explained to her husband and said", You have to stay with her only for six months. In return, we will get three lakh dollars. And you understand how much is three lakh dollars!

"I don't want her dollars", Anuj said, "I will not go anywhere leaving you"?

"Try to understand. In six months we will get more than two crore rupees. With this money we can buy our house and other things. You don't even need to do a job. You can start any work of your own".

"I said it. I will not leave you for money".

"I am saying that's why you will not go. Despite my refusal, you go on tour with the mistress of your company and live with her for many days".

Neerja explained to her husband, "If our future is made by living with Anichka, then what is wrong with it. A man's respect in the society is due to money".

"What will you say to people? Will you say that you sold your husband for money"?

"Why would I say so? Only three of us know this thing", Neerja said, "Do people not go abroad for jobs. You have also gone".

"You can give as many arguments as you want. I will not listen to you".

"Do you love me? Neerja asked.

"You also know, I love you more than my life".

"If you really love me, you will definitely listen to me".

Anuj did not want to go but had to bow down to his wife's insistence. He agreed to go with Anichka.

# XIV

"After all you have succeded in separating me from my wife". Anuj said to Anichka who was sitting next to him in the plane.

"I am not separating you from your wife. I am taking you with me only for six months" After listening to Anuj, Anichka said, "After six months you return to your wife".

"If people come to know about this, they will say that he left his wife for money and went to live with another women ".

"People will get a chance to say this when they come to know about this, " Anichka said, " Only I, you and your wife know this. When none of us will say this, then how will people know".

"People will guess when I'm with you in your house".

"Don't worry ,I will keep you as my private secretary. So that people don't get chance to make. things up".

After a long flight , Anuj reached her home in Los Angeles with Anichka.

Where is Anichka's luxurious bungalow and where is Anuj's small reuted house. Anuj was stunned to see the grandeur of Anichka's bungalow. Now Anuj had to live in his bungalow with Anichka.

"This is your room", Anichka showing the room to Anuj said, "from today you are my personal secretary."

" You have made me your personal secretary but what should I do?"

"Answering people's letters after seeing the post. And you find yourself what you have to do?"

Anichka had many cars.She gave him a car and a driver so he can go anywhere?

Anuj had found many works on his own so that he could keep himself busy.

Anichka was working in many films simultaneously so her schedule was very busy.

Some times she would return late at night from shooting and sometime she would leave very early in the morning. but she did not forget to come to Anuj's room

Whenever she got time, She used to sit near Anuj. while talking to Anuj, she did not forget to ask two things.

First she asked, "you don't have any problem here. Secondly she do talk to Neerja every day. She is your wife. She should not feel that you have forgotten her by being near me.

Earlier, Anichka used to talk johnson on the phone daily.but after knowing his reality, she stopped calling him. If Johnson's call came , she would not picked up. And one day Johnson himself came when he came she was laughingly talking to Anuj.

"Who is he" ? Johnson said seeing the stranger near Anichka.

"Anuj".

"Who Anuj" ?

"Anuj is a resident of Mumbai. I have brought him with me".

"Why" ?

"He is living in live-in-relationship with me".

"You are married",

"I know"

"How can you live in a live-in-relationship with another man after being married" ?

"Like you're living with Nancy".

"I'm the man".

"If you're a man , I'm woman". A quarrel started between Anichka and Johnson regarding Anuj. Johnson wanted Anichka not to stay with Anuj. Throw him out of the house Anichka flatly refused to listen to Johnson. Then he became furious and spoke angrily, "If you don't take Anuj out of your house, the conseqences will be bad".

Johnson left after threatening Anichka

"It is better, I get out of here".

"Why"?

My being with you is spoiling the relationship between husband and wife".

"Relations had deteriorated on the same day when I came to know about Johnson's exploits knowing his reality, I have hated him". Opening Johnson's black book, Anichka said, "I do not want to have a relationship with such a man".

"Here divorce is easily available. When you don't want to have a relationship with Johnson, then why don't you take a divorce"?

"I will divorce and definitely. It is better to live without a husband than to be the wife of such a dissolute man". Anichka said in harsh voice, "He says I am a man, whatever I do Before giving divorce, I want to tell him that if a woman also comes to her mind she can do anything. Haven't you seen? I have replied to him in his own language, so how did he get upset?

One day Anichka was going for a shoot. The car was being driven by the driver. Suddenly, a truck came from the wrong direction and hit the car. Collision was so severe that the car was completely shattered. The driver was badly injured. Anichka was sitting behind. Yet she was also badly hurt. Thank God her life was saved. The Police took them both to the hospital.

As soon as Anuj got the news of the accident he rushed to the hospital without a moment delay. Anichka was badly injured. Her hand and leg were fractured. Anichka had to stay in the hospital for a week. Anichka's arms and legs were plastered.

Anuj stayed with Anichka like a shadow in the hospital. Anuj brought Anichka home after discharged from the hospital.

"Anuj, keep a nurse". Anichka had spoken on coming home.

"Why"?

"To take care of me".

"There is no need for a nurse", Anuj said, "I am".

Anichka advised Anuj to have a nurse, but he refused.

Anichka's arms and legs were plastered. So she lay in bed. Anuj used to change her clothes, give her medicine and feed her.

Anuj united day and night to serve and care for Anichka. And after forty days the plaster on Anichka's hands and feet was cut off.

"Along with oil massage and fomentation, exercise will also have to be done", After cutting the plaster, the doctor had advised what to do?

"Now keep a nurse". On coming home. Anichka had once again told Anuj, "For oil massage, fomentation and exercise",

"You don't seen to trust me"?

"Don't say that. If you were not here? I don't know what would have happened to me today", Anichka said expressing him gratitude towards Anuj, "You have been serving me for so many days. You must also be tire. If you hire a nurse, you will also get rest".

"I'll be at ease the day you're all right". And Anuj again refused to hire a nurse.

Anuj used to massage oil on Anichk's hand and feed and trains also, Made her exercises and held her hand and made her walk.

One day when Anuj was making her walk, Anichka said, "Neerja is very lucky".

"Why"?

"She's got a husband like you".

"Such is the relation of husband and wife. Both are companions of each other sorrows and happiness. Devoted to each other".

"Husband is mine too".

The truck that hit Anichk's car and ran away, was not yet caught by the police. But Anichka was sure that Johnson was behind the accident. She was a super star. As soon as the news of the accident with her came in the media, people's phones started coming to see her and ask about her well being. Her fans started wishing her a speedy recovery.

But Johnson neither called nor came to see her. This convinced Anichka that he was behind the accident.

Time moves. It moves. At its own pace. Uninterrupted, unceasing, uninterrupted, not stop.

Anichka was completely cured by Anuj's night and day service and care. She started walking like before. She was so impressed by Anuj's dedication that one day she took him in her arms and kissed him, "If you weren't...

Before Anichka's unexpected behavior, Anuj was taken aback, but when he looked into her eyes, he too embraced her...

Due to Anichka's accident, the shooting of the films, she was working on was halted. Producers were overjoyed when Anichka made a full recovery.

Due to the accident, the producers of her films were suffering a lot. That's why she wanted the films to be completed as soon as possible. So she started shooting day and night. She was so busy that she had not time to talk to Anuj. One day while leaving for the shoot, Anichka went to Anuj's room and spoke to him, "Six months were about to be complete".

"Yes. I know".

Anichka did not talk to Anuj for several days due to being busy with the shooting. Neerja was also eagerly waiting for her husband to return. Whenever she spoke to Anuj her eagerness was reflected in her words.

"This is your ticket". One day Anichka said giving ticket to Anuj, "You have to go next week".

When months had passed, how hard was it to pass a week.

And the day has come for Anuj to return to Mumbai. Anichka had called Neerja before leaving for the airport, "Neerja I am sending your husband back to you as per my promise".

Anichka had spoken before leaving the house. "Take this".

"What is this"? Anuj said looking at Anichka.

"Cheque for two lac dollars".

"Sorry I didn't talk about money with you" Anuj refused to accept the cheque.

"You have already given Neerja what you promise her".

"You are right. I have given money to Neerja as per my promise", Anichka said, "But I am giving this to you out of my pleasure".

"Sorry". Anuj did not take money from Anichka even after many requests. Anichka did farewell to Anuj at the airport, "You will not forget me after going to your wife"?

"I am so lucky that I got an opportunity to be with a superstar like you. I am taking back all the beautiful memories of your time with me", Anuj taking Anichka's hand in his said, "These memories will always be in my hears".

"Anuj even I will not be able to get out of my heart".

And Anuj was gone.

# XV

"Anuj".

As soon as Anuj came out of the terminal, Neerja called him. She was very happy to see her husband after a long time.

"Neerja", seeing his wife, Anuj smilingly came to her and took her in his arms and asked, "How are you"?

"Fine", Neerja said, "And you"?

"Look me". Standing in front of you".

"And Anichka"?

"Completely healthy now. Busy in shooting".

"How was your time? What did you do all day"?

"Will you do all these things or will you go home too"?

"Sorry". She had met her husband after so many days so she forget. When Anuj spoke, she realized her mistake and said,

"Come". Neerja took her husband hand and brought him with her to a car parked in the parking stand. Then after taking the trolley bag from his hand and keeping it in the trunk of the car, she opened the door of the car and said "Sit".

"Whose car is it"? Anuj said while sitting in the car.

"Own".

"You brought a car"?

"Yes", Neerja said sitting on the driving seat, "And had also learned to drive a car".

And the car started moving. Anju had came to Mumbai after six months. Today, this same roads which he had passed many times, seemed strange to him. It was he had come back from a less populated city to a more populous city. The streets were crowed. Along with driving the car, Neerja was also talking to her husband. Along with telling her news, she was also asking her husband about his news.

"Where are you going here"? Anuj interrupted his wife, "Our house is this side".

"Don't worry. You are mine. I will not take you to someone else's house. I will take you to my own house".

And in other words, it was not even known when the car stopped in front of a house in the gated colony.

"Come", Neerja got down from the car and said to her husband. When Anuj came out of the car, she took him by the hand and took him inside the house and said, "Now this house is ours".

Neerja had asked her husband after showing the whole house, "How is the new house"?

"Very nice", Anuj said appreciating the choice of his wife, "You bought a house too, That too wonderful".

Along with telling her husband about herself, Neerja was also asking her husband about Anichka and America.

"I have lost my job", Anuj told his wife, "Now I have to find another job"?

"You don't need to search for another job".

"Why"? Anuj had asked.

"We will start our own business".

"What work"?

"You have just come back. Take rest for a few days. Let's think whatever it will be right to work".

Neerja and Anuj, after thinking for several days, took a shop on rent. In this shop, along with cosmetic and women's goods, photostat, lamination and stationery items were kept.

And slowly their shop started running. The salary that Anuj did not get for working in the company, he started earning more from the shop. Both husband and wife used to manage the shop.

After returning from America, Anuj neither called Anichka nor received her call. Anuj had returned from Anichka to his wife. He was living with his wife. But Anichka was not forgotten. Every moment he used to miss her.

Several months passed after returning from America. One day Anuj's mobile phone rang. As soon as he put the phone to his ear, a voice came, "I Anichka...

"Say Anichka"?

"Come soon"...

Anuj kept saying hello but the phone was disconnected Anuj dialed the phone again. The phone kept ringing but Anichka did not pick up the phone.

"What is the matter"? Looking at husband, Neerja said, "Whose phone was it " ?

"Anichka".

"Anichka", Neerja spoke after hearing the name of Anichka, "What was she saying"?

"Called me immediately".

"Why did she call you"? You didn't ask"?

"She disconnected the call by saying come soon".

"Try calling again".

"I have done it many times. Now she is not picking up the phone", Anuj spoke, "Hearing her voice it seemed that she is quite nervous".

"There must be some issue, so you have been called immediately", Neerja said to her husband, "She had faith in you, That is why she had called you. You should go".

On the advice of her wife Anuj left for America the same night. Throughout the flight, he kept thinking about Anichka. What is the matter? Why has she been called him immediately.

In this turmoil, Anuj reached Los Angeles after travelling a long way. When he reached Anichka's bungalow from the airport, he came to know that Anichka is in the hospital.

Anuj had reached the hospital.

"What happened to you"? Seeing Anichka's condition Anuj got upset, "I had left you absolutely safe. Then how did you become like this.

Anuj started crying after seeing the condition of Anichka.

"Anuj, you have come", Anichka said taking Anuj's hand in hers, "I was sure that you would definitely come".

A lot of things are published in the print media about heroes and heroined affair...Love...breakup and don't know what. Half of them are reality and half are hoaxes. People read such news with glee. Fame is also available. That's why they ignore the wrong things too.

A lot was printed about Anichka also. But not about Johnson because he was not a celebrity. But after marrying Anichka, he also became a celebrity. Before marriage about Anichka affair with other hero etc. But after Anichka's marriage to Johnson, their love affair, honeymoon etc were published.

Earlier Johnson was known only to a few people. But after his marriage to Anichka people also came to know him.

Earlier stories of Anichka and Johnson's love were published. But only a few days after their marraige, the news of the tenison in their marriage life started getting published. And the Journalists had discovered Johnson's past which was not discovered before.

Johnson was married and living with another woman. And to teach him a lesson. Anichka had also decided to live with Anuj. Anichka had not told anyone that she was living in a live-in-relationship with Anuj. But don't know how journalists got wind of this.

Anichka did not want to live with Johnson. She had taken the decision to divorce him. But first she wanted to answer Johnson in his own language. So she stayed with Anuj. And as soon as Anuj left, she filed a case of divorce.

Anichka is getting divorced, this news was causing a lot of defamation to Johnson. The exploists of Johnson were not known to the world before. The reason for Anichka's divorce was revealed to the people. People considered Johnson to be decent and respectable. But as soon as the mask was removed from the face, his real face came in front of the people.

Johnson was getting a lot of bad name in the society. He called Anichka. But she had stopped picking up Johnson's call long ago. He kept on calling for several days. When Anichka's phone did not pick up he reached Los Angeles one day.

"Madam is not at home". The guard said on seeing Johnson.

"Where is she"?

"Germany for outdoor film shooting".

"When will she return"?

"One month later".

And Johnson was back. He kept on finding out and when Anichka returned then one day he came again.

"You". Anichka spoke on sight of Johnson.

"Yes. I".

"Why are you here"?

"Explain to you".

"Explain to me", Anichka said, "What have you come to explain to me"?

"You take back the divorce case. Your divorce case is giving me a lot of bad name in the society. You don't wnat to stay with me. Don't stay. What is the need to bring the court in between. We break up the relationship only by mutual consent".

"I don't want to with a lustful man like you even for a moment. I want to break up with you. legally", Anichka said angrily after listening to Johnson, "You go away from here. Otherwise I will push you out".

"Won't go", Johnson said, " I am asking for the last time. Whether you will take back the divorce case or not"?

"You are asking for the last time, So I am also answering you for the last time", Anichka spoke, "Not at all".

"If the case is not withdrawn, then you will not live in this world either".

"Threatening me".

"Take it as a threat", Johnson said angrily, "Will you be mine or not"?

"No...No...Never...".

Johnson was furious when he 'did not' listen to Anichka. He has brought a pistol. He fired a volley of bullets at Anichka. Hearing the gunshots, servants and guards came running. Johsnon shot himself before they could catch him.

"Nothing will happen to you. You will be fine". Anuj's heart started crying after hearing about the incident with Anichka.

"Don't cry Anuj. Death cannot be avoided by crying or by false consolation. Even after so many bullets I am still breathing. Do you know why I am still alive"?

After listening to Anichka, Anuj started looking at her face with questioning eyes.

"I am waiting for you", Anichka said, "Nurse".

The nurse took the signal of Anichka and brought the newborn. She gave the baby to Anichka. Anichka gave the baby to Anuj and said, "Hold your sign".

"Sign". Anuj looking at the baby said.

"Your baby girl".

"My baby girl". Anuj looked at Anichka with astonishment.

"Forgot the day that happened between us". When Anichka reminded him, the scene of that day flashed before Anuj's eyes.

Anichka said kissing Anuj in her arms when she was completely healthy, "If you were not"?

Anuj was taken aback by Anichka's unexpected behaviour and looked at her with astonishment.

"What are you looking like"? Anichka kissed him once again.

Anuj had been living with Anichka for a long time but this was the first time. He looked into Anichka's eyes and read the language of her eyes. he too gained courage and took Anichka in his arms and kissed her.

"You"...

And when the bodies of Anuj and Anichka came closer their breath started heating up and the distance between their bodies disappeared. The two bodies became one.

"Anuj, our daughter is a sign of what happened between us that day". Anichka said, "You wanted a daughter like me. This is our daughter. She will always remind you of me".

And Anichka's life flew away. She was still breathing while waiting for Anuj.